A Lovely,
Indecent Departure

A Novel

Steven Lee Gilbert

This book is a work of fiction. Names, characters, places and incidents are either products of the author's imagination or are used fictitiously. Any resemblance to actual events or locales or persons, living or dead, is entirely coincidental

Copyright © 2012 by Steven Lee Gilbert

ISBN 978-0-9853365-0-9

Cover design © by Lee Warchal
Author Photograph © Stacey Kaufman

www.stevenleegilbert.com

For Franca, naturally

A Lovely,
Indecent Departure

Book I

-Custody

Look, there comes the girl. She is treading alone up the sidewalk. Looking like anyone else of the noontime crowd blissfully strolling the strip mall. But she is not one of them, and never has been.

See how she clutches her purse to her chest, how her eyes are guarded and watchful. See how her footsteps fall slow and deliberate, like a leery but obedient child. She knows no one's paying her attention, still she watches them and watches their faces. She is watching for signs of trouble, though she's not expecting any, she's just there to use the pay phone. But if someone happened to recognize her, a student perhaps or a parent, when word of what she'd done had spread they might remember this fact and forward it on to police, who could then check telephone records. See how she makes her way slowly amongst them, like some trespasser over them all, trying hard not to look in a hurry. Watch how those people she meets on the street move about her like she'd never existed. See, that suits the girl just fine. She was born and raised in a poor hillside town in northern Italy, an only child whom her father had abandoned and whose mother had worked two jobs. She's felt invisible all of her life.

The day is gray and breezy, with a forecast for wet weather. Already, to the south of town, just beyond the river and past the tall white steeple of the seminary school where the mountains rise out of the foothills, a purple-grey menacing barrier has supplanted the high ridge-line and obscures the horizon in haze. The air shouldered down smells of rain. It is winter, loathe to let go.

Beyond the last of the shops and across the two lane road a man sits atop a tractor, steering it down a worn dirt track, his eyes burrowed beneath his ball cap. He is following the fencerow where the road has been cut through his pasture and carrying a load of baled hay for the cluster of cows which are standing just up the hill huddled against the dreary, ash-colored sky. The animals dotting the slope are all pointed in his direction. Cars passing by. Someone honks. Without looking up, the farmer raises one gloved hand and bids them hello.

The girl understands his resolve. One of the hardest things in the world to accept is uninvited change. It is her own reason for being there.

When she comes to the place where the sidewalk ends she finds a fat bearded man in dirty white coveralls is using the only pay phone. She looks at her watch and then steps to the side and stands waiting, holding her purse in both hands. A thin, olive-skinned woman with straight black hair, dressed in jeans and a white turtleneck, and wearing a brown suede jacket.

The man appears not to notice her. He is talking loudly and gesturing with his free hand, his shoulder set firmly against the brick wall, and his lunch is arrayed on the phone's narrow shelf. When he finishes with what he has to say he pinches the phone in the crook of his fat, hairy neck and skins what is left of the half eaten sandwich from the flimsy container and angling it just so shoves it wholly into his mouth. His cheeks bulge as if filled with air. Speckles of orange pimento cheese adhere to his beard and mustache. As he strokes a hand across his mouth and chin brushing away bits of the food, finally his eyes wash over her.

She finds in them an unsettling sentiment and turns away. She is thinking of going elsewhere when a large pickup truck full of men pulls up to the curb. The driver lays on the horn and the man on the phone looks over at them, in reply lifts a middle finger. The driver honks again, this time longer and she looks at the men in the truck. Four white, scruffy faces gaze back at her with a mixture of disinterest and appetite from beneath their varied ball caps. The man hangs up the phone and swinging his hips ostentatiously sashays over and climbs in the cab and the girl watches them go. She walks over and stops and stands looking at the phone. She stands there a very long time. Her arms hang limp at her side. Then extending one hand past the trash left behind she picks up the telephone.

A man answers the call. Pronto.

Alfredo, she says.

Sì.

It's me, Anna.

Anna? Oh, Anna, sì, sì. Come stai, Anna!

Sto' bene, Alfredo.

He starts to say something else but she cuts him off. I don't have much time, Alfredo, she says, speaking English to sharpen her uncle's appreciation for where she is calling from. Are you ready? she asks.

Silence, then: Per cosa?

Vengo.

Adesso?

She hesitates. Sì, adesso, she says. Oggi. *Today*.

Ma Anna, he begins, but again she stops him.

I can't wait any longer.

Do you have him?

No, she interjects, not wanting him to say the name. She looks behind her. She lowers her voice. I pick him up this evening.

Are you sure of this? he asks. You know what you are doing?

Yes, she says, but she doesn't. You can hear it in her voice. Are you going to help me or not? she asks.

Another brief second of silence passes before her uncle answers, his voice low and solemn. Sì, Anna, he says. Vieni. I will meet you in Genova.

By mid-afternoon it had started to rain. She stood at her classroom window watching the buses line up outside where the teachers were ushering the children around from beneath oversized umbrellas. Beyond the loading and unloading zone the staff parking lot had already begun to empty. She looked for her small blue car and then glanced at the clock on the wall. She walked over and sat at her desk where she'd gathered student work to occupy her until it was time for her to leave.

The art room was on the lower level, along with a couple of other electives, and as such out of the way. Only the janitor and one fellow teacher even noticed her working late. When the shop teacher stuck his head in the doorway and announced it was time to get out of there she startled. She looked at him. His lunch cooler was slung over one shoulder, hanging by a strap, and there were tiny bits of sawdust clinging to his clothes and in his hair. One of his pants' leg had gotten hung up in the laces of his tall work boots.

Just trying to wrap up a few things, she replied.

He nodded and glanced down the hall. He looked awkward to be standing there and she noticed that he was holding what appeared to be a wooden bowl in his hands. Behind her the rain pelted the window. He looked at the window and said, Feels like snow, doesn't it?

I sure hope not, she said.

Is it supposed to?

Just rain, I think, the last I'd heard.

He nodded and looked down at the bowl. He seemed to have forgotten he was holding it. Oh, this is for you, he said. He walked over and handed it to her. The bowl was smooth and solid in her hands, you could see the different grains of the pieces of wood that had gone in to making it. It's just something I made, he said.

She looked at him. He was grinning.

He said, Teaching the kids how to use the lathe. He pointed to the bowl awkwardly. I thought you might be able to fit a small flower pot in there. Or mail, or spare change, the TV remote. Things like that.

Thank you, she said and she looked at him and looked at the bowl and she set it down on the desk and looked up at him again.

Anyway, he said and he smiled and shoved both hands in his back pockets and then took them out again and shrugged and started backing toward the door. Enjoy your weekend. Enjoy the bowl.

I will. Thank you again.

That sounded stupid, didn't it? Who tells someone to enjoy a bowl?

She shook her head and though she didn't want to she smiled too. Really, she said, it was kind of you.

Their eyes locked briefly and then he looked at the rain-streaked window and said, Well, I guess I'll leave you to it. I'm going to get out of here in case that forecast of yours is wrong.

I'll be right behind you, she said, but once he was gone she went back to her work.

The projects did little to occupy her and her mind drifted again and again to the wooden bowl and was further agitated by the shop teacher's suggestion of snow. She had not planned on snow. The mountains at night would be treacherous. With just under an hour to go before she had intended to leave she closed the grade book and placed it in the center of her desk where it would be easily found then she gathered her purse from the bottom desk drawer and walked to the classroom door.

She flipped off the light and turned back and took in the room one last time. The room looked lonely, dark and austere. Something Van Gogh might've painted for the room's emotional honesty. Or Hemingway, had he been a Post-Impressionist painter and not a writer, for its stark nakedness.

She wondered of the children's reactions. Would any of them understand, or even care, as they filed into the classroom on Monday, their voices exuberant and unrestrained, going on about this or that, of their weekend and of things unrelated to school, and then having found their seats turn to face her desk and feeling an instant of jubilation as they realized she was not there, enjoying a few more minutes of freedom when still she didn't appear, then slowly their jubilance turning to question and finally conjecture, until one of them, most likely Rebecca Sylvester, would stand and hurry with haste down the hall to the office and ask where was their teacher?

The man entered from the hall and when he saw the boy sitting alone at a table in a corner of the room reading a book it pleased his father so to see his son off to himself behaving while the other few children who remained at the daycare center were playing wildly and darting about. He looked for and found his teacher by her large round bottom where she stood bent at the waist wiping the nose of a curly, blonde-haired girl. He looked back at the boy, who had spotted him already and closed the book and was returning it to the bookshelf. Then he walked over and knelt at the cubbies where the backpacks and jackets were kept and started packing his things up. His father met him there.

You ready? he asked.

The boy nodded.

The man looked up and saw the teacher was headed their way, then a cry alerted her to a scuffle erupting between two boys from across the room and she scampered after them with a wave. The boy stood and hoisted his Disney backpack on his shoulders.

Don't forget your jacket, Evan told him.

The boy grabbed the windbreaker and they were turning to leave just as the teacher finally made her way over. All set? she asked.

They looked at her. Neither of them spoke.

Don't forget, the girl said, we're off to the zoo next Tuesday. I don't think we've got Oliver's permission slip yet. Is he planning to go?

I think so, the man replied.

I mentioned it to your wife, too, this morning. Which reminds me. The girl looked down at the boy. Did you remember your card?

I almost forgot, the boy answered and he hurried over to one of the counters where he searched through the things lying there until he picked up a sheet of red construction paper and carried it back to the door.

What's that? his father asked when it was just the two of them out in the hall.

Just something I made, said the boy and he tucked it away in his backpack and started off toward the door.

She stood at the door in the drizzly mess waiting for someone to answer. Inside she heard Oliver call her name. Not Mommy, not Mom, but her name, and though the sound of his voice should have thrilled her, it filled her mind with fury.

Footsteps approached the door and the door creaked as if a weight were pressing against it. The blinds covering the window shuddered once then stopped. She pushed a strand of damp hair from her face and waited and watched as two delicate fingers appeared at the side of the sash. They peeled back the blind from the window and one tiny green eye peered out. The girl smiled and started to wave then another voice called out and the fingers suddenly recoiled.

Anna straightened and stared open-mouthed at the door. She could hear the two of them talking, her son and his father, but she couldn't make out their words or even what manner of insult and fear her ex-husband preferred in convincing their only child to downgrade her status to that of a friend of the family. But of course it was the reaction he wanted from her, her ex-husband, that devil: anger, misery, madness. He would come when he would come, Evan that is, and of all the things she did now, standing at her son's father's door, waiting for it to open, infuriated her the most.

The house had once belonged to her. She'd picked out those very blinds. She knew intently every square inch of this home they'd shared together.

His arrogance dumfounded her. Children go where they are pointed.

It was really no different than when they were married, wretched wetness and all. She'd been divorced from him for over two years and she could still feel his opposing authority, his criticism and insult.

The storm stepped itself up a notch and altered its course from a drizzle to a slight downpour. In the distance thunder rose to a roar and lightning flashed nearby, piercing the swollen sky and reflecting off the silver underbellies of the turned up leaves of the young silver maples she'd planted along the drive. She glared at the heavens, then at the door and her heart stopped momentarily at the thought of being struck dead outside of this house of all places.

The awning covering the porch stoop was small and narrow and the stoop itself barely wide enough to stand upon and made even less inviting by a cluster of head-dead potted plants and when she stepped beneath it her foot struck a potted container and she watched horrified as the plant teetered then tumbled over the edge, shattering on the driveway and spilled the fern and its dried black soil onto the wet pavement.

Well, shit, she muttered and stared down at the other dead plants, which looked to her poorly rooted in soil that lacked nutrients. Children and ex-wives, it seemed, were not the only victims of Evan's neglect.

The bastard was probably watching her now, she thought. Shit-eating grin all over his face, like the weather was all his doing. Then she pounded again on the door.

Go get your stuff, Evan said to the boy and he looked down and checked his wrist watch. Ten minutes to six. She was early again and it was raining, so he didn't mind her having to wait. He looked again at the boy. Do as I said, he scolded when he saw he hadn't moved.

Evan peered again through the blinds. She was watching it rain and getting wet and he could sense the anger rising in her and that gave him some satisfaction. Then as the rain fell harder, came that familiar stirring in his groin as the rainwater soaked through her white turtleneck, giving rise to a pair of poorly concealed, dark Mediterranean nipples.

The boy came running back in the room and asked, Can I take my Game Boy?

Does it belong here?

You got it for me.

Then it belongs here. *House Rules.*

The boy ran off again and he turned back to the slit in the blinds and saw with mixed emotion that the rain had driven her beneath the awning. She looked up at the door and he watched her and he reached down and shifted himself through the fabric of his chinos, allowing his hand to linger.

Enjoying the view?

He turned. Angela was standing in the doorway to the kitchen, resting her hands on her hips.

What view? he asked. There came another knock on the door.

That one, she said. Would you like to invite her in?

He didn't answer and stepped away from the door and he turned his back to her and slipped sideways into the hall.

That is his ride, isn't it? Angela called out.

Evan found the boy in his room, holding a plastic grocery sack. Let's see, he said and he took the bag and peered inside and saw that it was stuffed with the clothes he'd worn home from her house the last time. Pants, shirt, underwear. And one last thing: the cherry red sheet of construction paper he'd seen him bring home from preschool.

What is this anyway? he asked.

It's her birthday card. I made it for her at school.

Her birthday's not for another two weeks.

I wanted to give it to her now.

He watched the boy's face as he stuffed the card into his pants pocket. Here, give her these, he said and he scooped up a handful of classwork from the dresser top and stuffed them in on top of the clothes. He tied the bag shut. I'll drop the card off in the mail tomorrow.

But—

No buts. She can get it in the mail.

I don't mail you your birthday card.

You do hers.

Not this Mom's either.

He was done talking about it. He shoved the bag at the boy. Now go say good-bye to your mother.

Where is she?

I don't know. Find her.

He followed behind as the boy slunk out of the room. He told him not to open the door until he got there and then he went across the hall and into the opposite room where he pulled the piece of card stock from his pocket and read what his son had written. When he had finished he looked over his shoulder toward the door and then walked over to the corner of the room near the desk. He fed the card into the shredder attached to the rim of the trash can and turned and walked back to the hall.

Oliver was standing with his back against the kitchen door, smiling broadly, ready, it seemed, as if about to piss his pants.

Evan looked at his watch. Two minutes till. Not on the mark but close enough. He waved the boy out of the way. Step back, he said. I'll open it.

The door finally opened and she glared at him fiercely and asked where was her son.

I'm here. I'm here, the boy said, and he emerged, carrying his things in a plastic grocery bag, not the pretty Mickey Mouse backpack she'd given him. He wedged his way around his father's tall, bone-narrow frame.

She smiled at him and squatted and spread her arms wide, but just as the boy was about to step into them his father reached down and stopped him. He clamped down on his shoulder.

First things first, Evan said. You need to see if you can't do a better job of getting him back on time.

Don't start with that, she replied. She looked at Oliver and smiled at him.

Maybe if you followed the rules I wouldn't have to remind you of them.

She didn't answer and Evan glanced away and noticed the broken planter. His eyes hardened as they turned on her. The order says six o'clock, he said.

I know what the order says. She looked at him and stood.

Do you?

Yes, I do.

There came a sound then from behind her and they looked across the drive, which was shared by the house next door. There, a little dark-haired toddler was standing in the doorway wearing only a diaper and banging a sucker against the glass. A large, yellow tomcat circled her legs. The girl wrinkled her nose and grinned, her teeth spilling out of her gums like crooked white roadside markers stained red from the lollipop. Hands then reached out from behind the girl and an older woman, her blue-gray hair in pink rollers, stepped out of the dark interior and glaring at her through the storm door, nudged the cat with her slippered foot and pulled the child backwards. She slammed the door behind her.

Anna looked sadly at Oliver. He smiled at her and she smiled back and she looked up and glared at his father. We're leaving, she said. Let him go.

Evan relaxed his grip and the boy flung himself at her legs. She put her arms around him.

He has something Sunday afternoon, Evan said.

She looked at him. Has what?

Something on Sunday.

I heard that. What does he have I'm asking?

He didn't answer her right away. It's private, he said. Just with family.

Whatever. As long as it's after six.

It's at two.

He can't make it then.

He'll need to be home by then.

The order says six o'clock. You just said that.

These are extenuating circumstances.

I don't care.

It's his aunt's birthday. She's having a party and he asked to be there.

She stared at him and then looked down at the boy. Is that true? she asked.

Oliver didn't answer.

We'll see you at six on Sunday, she said to Evan and bent down to pick the boy up.

Actually, it's not his decision, Evan said.

She looked up at him. And you think it's yours?

It doesn't matter what I think. It's what the judge thinks.

She could think of nothing to say and so turned her eyes and looked out at what she could see of the tiny backyard. The playset and swing, parts of it rusted and weatherworn. Oliver's sandbox. The overgrown remnants of her vegetable garden, where what had become of her efforts there the same as what had become of her life, and her son's, too: a tangled and unsettling mess.

She looked at Evan and he looked the same to her, more age around the eyes, his hair showed signs of thinning, but his figure stood tall, lean and healthy. Still handsome, but she saw nothing attractive about him. Only hatred and bitterness.

She bent down to one knee and scooped the boy up in her arms and shielding him from the falling rain she wasted not another minute and hurried with him to the car. She buckled him in. I missed you so much, she said.

Me, too, Mommy.

She stroked his hair. All set?

He nodded and she shut his door and hustled around to the driver's side and started the engine and she put the car in reverse. It wasn't until they'd backed down the drive that she gave the house a final glance. Evan was standing half-out in the doorway, watching them depart, his face hollow of any emotion.

Wave good-bye to your dad, she said to the boy, who wasn't paying him any attention. She watched in the rearview mirror as he leaned toward the window and waved and she started off down the street, satisfied then that she'd done all she could to allow for the proper parting between this father and his son.

Book II

-Monroe

The sheriff Monroe Rossi stood back from the edge of the pond in the bloodroot and tall mountain oat grass and looked over the feral brushland listening for the Spaniels. The two dogs made plenty of noise, their splash and the sound of their traipse through the meadow so youthful and indiscriminate not even the company of mallards floating in the green murky water appeared threatened by the pups' presence. Mostly the dogs stuck to the thicket and undergrowth testing their knowledge of turkey and quail, an affinity for which they and their owner both suffered.

When the scent led the pups through the sagging fence row and into the hardwood forest Monroe turned and walked up the hill past the woodpile and past the stacks of sodden rotting lumber and he picked up and followed the faint channel of a footpath over to the crumbling foundation where a house had once stood. He stopped and propped one booted foot on the fallen stones and hung his head momentarily, looking himself like a relic of bygone better days.

At the sound of an engine he turned and looked up the hill toward the road where a sporty black coupe came creeping over the rise. The car slowed to a stop alongside the Blazer where he'd parked it in the weeds at the edge of the road and Monroe listened closely for voices but could not hear any. After a minute or so the engine revved and the car went up and around the bend.

Monroe looked at the Blazer. He could see the outline of the girl sitting in the front seat, her eyes pointed straight ahead, what she was thinking was anyone's guess. Whatever teenagers thought these days.

One of the dogs bawled and he turned and looked just as the two of them came crashing back through the thicket at a low place in the field. Their noses were pressed to the ground in pursuit of what he knew not, a vestige of something familiar, and he whistled at them and the two of them lifted their heads and their eyes searched the hillside for him. When they found him they came running and he noted the grace in their stride, their long legs, how they covered the ground without seeming to touch it and the way their mouths hung open and their tongues flattened and hung to the side. They came up and he told them to sit and they did, sat quivering at his feet, gazing up at him with their bright, hazel eyes, then he bent and patted the sides of them which were matted and wet and covered in cockleburs and he said to them both, Good girl, and then straightened and started back up the hill toward the Blazer, the two pups bounding ahead of him.

When he came to the edge of the road he stopped. Beyond was the cemetery. He dropped the tailgate and reached in and pulled out the shovel and a flat of pansies and set them on the ground. He told the dogs to get in and they did. Before shutting them in he reached into his pants pocket and handed them each a dog biscuit, then he slammed the gate shut and walked up toward the front of the vehicle. He stopped at the driver's side door and peered in. You coming?

The girl didn't answer.

Rebecca?

She looked up from the stack of school books in her lap and glared with a smugness at him. He waited for her to take out her earplugs and when she didn't he wiggled his finger at his own ear. She reached up and tugged one free. Are you coming? he asked.

She looked back at down at her lap. I'm studying.

He looked at the books and saw they were closed but didn't say anything back to her right away, he just stood there looking in at her with his hands on the rim of the door. How long you planning to stay mad at me? he asked.

How long until you start treating me like an adult?

I treat you fair for a fifteen year old.

Sure you do.

He glanced toward the back where the two dogs were laying on their sides, breathing heavily. He looked at her again. All this just because of a party?

It was a school tradition. I should have been allowed to go.

It was a party. Just because you change the name of something doesn't change what it is. Besides, it was at the Bowman's? Don't think I don't know what goes on over there.

She rolled her eyes. Right. I forgot you're the sheriff. You know everything that goes on everywhere.

I also find it hard to believe that your mother said you could go.

So now I'm a liar to boot.

Listen, he said, I'm done talking about this.

I believe you're the one who brought it up.

Are you coming or not?

Rebecca didn't answer. She re-fitted her earphone and and opened a book and lowered her eyes.

Monroe turned to go, then he turned back to ask her, Who was that anyway, in the car?

Don't worry, she said, not looking up. It wasn't one of those horny Bowman boys stopping to show me his penis.

Monroe watched her. Then he left her alone with her anger and her surliness and he walked to the rear of the Blazer and he picked the shovel and the flowers and started across the blacktop.

The family cemetery lay a hundred feet off the road at the end of a narrow footpath in a small wooded grove, it was set off from the pastureland by a chain-link fence. He stood with his hands on the fence, looking over the cluster of old headstones. Weathered. Cracked. Shit-upon. On all but two were the names of ancestors all but unknown to him. Of the two he knew only one of them, his mother's, was inscribed with a date of death.

He opened the metal latch and came inside and walked over to where his mother—and eventually would his father—lay buried. Someone had placed a pot of yellow chrysanthemums before her headstone and the flowers lay on their side and had started to brown and wilt. He set the container upright and searched for a card or some other mention of who they were from but found nothing of any indication. He looked back at the Blazer. Then he stomped back through the gate and down the path to the car. Can you hand me that bottle of water? he asked when he came to the window.

Rebecca looked over at him and he pointed to it where it lay on the console between the two seats. She handed it to him. He was headed back across the road when the radio squawked.

Monroe stopped and listened and the radio squawked again and he turned around and walked over and opened the door and reached in and picked up the radio. Go ahead, Jeannie.

Sheriff?

Yeah, Jeannie, it's me.

Sorry, to bother you, Sheriff. I know you said no interruptions till you got in but I thought this shouldn't wait.

Monroe looked over the dash at the overgrown fencerow where near the top of the hill a woodchuck stood on its hind legs in the tall brush looking at them. What shouldn't?

Have you read today's paper?

No, not yet.

I didn't think so.

Why do you ask?

That reporter's piece, that's why.

Which reporter?

Jeffrey Barber.

Monroe glanced over at Rebecca and saw that she had spotted the wood chuck too and was watching it where it stood hunched at the edge of the road pawing at some trash. He thought of his office manager hunched over her desk, fuming over the paper she'd spread out before her like she did every morning. Jeannie, he said, this honestly sounds like it can wait.

He's already called here this morning asking for your comment.

That's fine.

What'll I tell him when he calls back, and you can bet he will call back?

You can tell him the same thing I told him last week.

He won't like that.

Well, it'll have to do.

He knows you can't talk about an ongoing investigation. You've told him that, right?

I've told him. Right now though I've got to go.

The rules don't change on account a there being an election. Speaking of which.

All right, Jeannie I really need to get off here. We're still at the cemetery, Rebecca and I. We've not stopped by the nursing home, and I've still got to drop the dogs off before getting her to her appointment on time.

Well, all right then. You tell her I said good luck.

I will.

She have fun at the Bowman's party this weekend?

Monroe hung his head. He looked at Rebecca. How'd you know about that? he asked Jeannie.

Know about it? Sheriff, the Bowman's bonfire is an Eden Hill High School tradition. Don't tell me you kept her from going.

Monroe hung up the radio without answering and as he was sliding out of the vehicle he glanced over at Rebecca, who was watching him with her eyes wide and gloating and her hands were lifted and palms turned up in a symbol of I-told-you-so.

Last chance, he said half heartedly, but he knew already that the way it was going this morning they were both way beyond second chances.

-Evan Meade

When he arrived downtown at the lot adjacent to the bank building it was almost nine. He went in through the side entrance and climbed the flight of stairs to the second floor where he walked in and shut the door to his small office. He sat down at his desk and opened the paper to the picture of his son and he sat looking at it and the article that accompanied it and when he heard the seminary clock tower across the river chime the top of the hour he folded the paper and set it aside and picked up the phone and dialed the telephone number.

Good Afternoon. FBI.

Agent Forster please.

Can I say who's calling?

Tell him it's Evan Meade.

Hold please, the woman snapped.

Evan rocked back in his chair. He swiveled around and looked out the window where the sun cast a golden-rose light on the upper-most floors and the blush creeping down the tall buildings illuminated the blue-shadowed street below. Across the street a construction crew was at work renovating the county jail. The pulse of a fully employed jackhammer surged upwards out of the earth where just beyond the erected chain link fence a group of men in hardhats were gathered around the equipment's lone operator.

Mr. Meade, what can I do for you today?

Evan turned to face the desk. I was wondering if you had a minute, he said.

As a matter of fact this is a bit of a bad time.

It won't take long.

The agent didn't respond right away. Can you hold for just a moment, he said and when he came back on the line he reported he'd cleared a few minutes. So, what's on your mind, Mr. Meade?

I was wondering, is there any word on Oliver?

Well, no, sir, there actually isn't. You know that as soon as we locate your son you'll be the first person we notify.

When do you think that might be?

I don't know that, Mr. Meade. His case is in the hands of a dozen different agencies that specialize in finding lost kids.

He's not lost.

I understand that. Those same agencies also track runaways, ransom kidnappings, kids that have just up and vanished.

He's not any of those things either.

I'm just saying, Mr. Meade, people are working on it.

Evan leaned forward on his elbows. A few more seconds passed until the agent finally relented. Mr. Meade, he said, I assure you, I have dozens of cases just like this. People are working around the clock to find your son. Are you there? Mr. Meade?

I'm here.

What I'm trying to say is we're using every available means.

Over the phone the agent then proceeded to re-commit all of the government's resources, the labs, the analysis, the investigators, all the qualified tools at his disposal. Evan stood and turned and faced the wall and he studied the decorative world map hanging there. He found Italy and starting at the toe he traced his way north, reading silently the city names on the poorly detailed atlas: Napoli, Roma, Firenze. To the right and higher up: Venezia and the Italian Alps; Milano and to the south of that, at a bend in the boot near the sea, he found Genova, written in bold, Gothic letters. He rested his eyes then his finger on an area just to the northeast of that spot where the town of San Salvatore would be if the shit-hole had been worth mentioning.

The agent was rambling on about something to do with Richmond, where they'd found her abandoned car. Cincinnati came next. He always ended with Cincinnati, that's where the trail grew cold, at a bus depot in Cincinnati.

Can I ask about San Salvatore? Evan said.

Sure. What about it?

Has anyone been back there? Have you talked any more to her family?

There's no firm evidence that your wife and son are or have ever been there.

But somebody there must know something.

Maybe. Unfortunately, there's only so much we can do in a foreign country. You'll have to trust me, Mr. Meade, we're doing all it is we can do.

Evan sat down. The door to his office opened and he looked up and saw Azim standing in the doorway.

Do you have the Gardner file? Azim asked.

Evan pointed and the older man stepped in and stood looking down at the pile of folders strewn about his desk. He looked up at Evan.

You can see I'm on the phone here, right? Evan asked him.

Azim paid no attention. He'd gone back to studying the desk. Where is it?

Right there. Evan leaned forward and pointed to a folder.

Azim gathered it up in his hands and he glanced inside. He looked at Evan. And the rest?

In the room.

Upstairs?

Yes, upstairs. Of course.

Azim took the file and left and Evan apologized to Forster and told him he needed to go.

Listen, Mr. Meade, I'm sorry I don't have anything new to give you at the moment. I do feel I should ask, though. Have you talked with anyone else about this?

Like who?

Like a private investigator.

You've led me to think that wouldn't be necessary. You said the FBI could handle it.

Well, yes sir, and I think that's exactly what we're doing. However, it might be, and please don't take this the wrong way, but it might be that you are expecting a quicker timetable than what the Bureau can deliver.

It's been six months.

Yes sir, I know how long it's been.

I just want them found.

Yes sir. I want that too.

But?

But with your wife's dual citizenship, her resources overseas, finding them is proving not to be easy and we knew it wouldn't be. Add to that certain international protocols that must be followed and you can see where a privatized agency might be better suited for the kind of turnaround you're expecting. Of course, those agencies come with a price, but if you'd like, there are several that specialize in international kidnappings, a couple right here in our state, I can get you their numbers if you'd be interested.

Evan closed his eyes. He leaned back in his chair while on the other end of the line the investigator searched his listings. His stomach turned with the menacing, noxious suspicion that Anna had gotten away with this and he'd seen them both for the very last time, as if all this time no one had even been looking.

He found Azim in his office flipping through the papers he'd taken from his desk. He rapped on the door. His boss looked up and saw who it was and went back to his work. What is it?

What's the problem with the Gardner account?

There's no problem.

Why all of the sudden the interest then?

Azim didn't answer. Tacked to the wall next to the desk was a large bank calendar. Someone had taken a red magic marker and circled Friday, the 21st. Evan started to ask him the question again when he heard a sound from behind him and turned just as Joyce stepped into the office. She was carrying a stack of files and he moved to the side to let her by and she sat them down on the desk.

That it? Azim asked.

That's all I could find, his admin said and she turned and nodded at Evan as she left.

Did he ask for this? Evan asked.

Who?

Him? Evan pointed with his chin at the file.

I haven't spoken with Philip Gardner.

Then is this about my son?

Azim finally stopped what he was doing and raised his head and peered over his glasses across the desk. He looked at Evan. The trouble with your son—

The trouble is with my ex-wife.

Azim corrected himself. The trouble with your ex-wife, I'm sure, has nothing to do with this.

The two men studied each other for another few seconds then Azim returned to his work and Evan returned to his office. He shut the door behind him. He sat down at his desk and he studied the note upon which he'd written the number the agent had given him, then he picked up the telephone.

-Monroe

It was mid-morning by the time they finished their errands and he pulled up to the steps of the high school. He set the Blazer in park and shut off the engine and started to get out.

You don't need to come in, Rebecca said. She had opened her book bag and was shoving the release forms she'd picked up at the doctor's office into one of the pockets.

Don't you need me to sign you in or something?

They don't do that.

He watched her. You ought not to just stuff that in there, he said.

She didn't answer.

What about that prescription?

What about it?

Do you need me to fill it for you?

She shook her head. I can get it later.

Won't you need it today?

She slung her book bag over her shoulder and stepped back from the car and looked at him. Dad, I have three other inhalers.

But are any of those for volleyball?

That's the one he just wrote a prescription for.

I know. Then let me fill it. I can drop it off later today.

It's fine, okay. I'll see you later. She shut the door and headed up the steps and he watched her go and after she was gone he left and drove the few blocks downtown past the jail to the temporary sheriff's annex they'd set up while the renovation work was being done. He parked out front and went inside. Hello? he called.

There was no answer and he walked behind the front counter and down the short hall to his office and as soon as he sat down behind the desk he saw the folded up newspaper someone had put there. He spread it open and flipped through it looking for the editorial section. He read it and afterwards he got up and went out to the counter and poured himself a cup of coffee and came back into the office and sat down and was browsing the other stories when he heard the front door open and someone come in. He set the paper aside.

Jeannie popped her head in the door. She held up a bumper sticker. A leader who listens? she asked.

Don't look at me. I'm not the one who came up with it.

Well, it just sounds phony. People need a sheriff who protects, not listens. It doesn't matter much if you hear them but can't do nothing about it.

They considered that, but it wouldn't all fit.

Jeannie wasn't amused. She noticed the paper laying on his desk. You read it? she asked.

Outside at the temporary duty officer's desk the radio station squawked. One of the auxiliaries working animal control came on requesting a radio check.

I did, Monroe replied.

What do you think?

I think people, especially people like Jeffrey Barber, will say whatever it is they want to.

The radio squawked again. Monroe spun the chair around and snatched up the receiver to his own radio and turned it on. Stokes, is that you?

Sheriff?

Where are you?

On my way to the campground, Sheriff.

Is that where you're supposed to be?

Yessir. Someone called in about some dogs chained up out here.

Monroe looked at Jeannie. Then get there, he said into the radio. And hold the radio chatter.

He set the radio down on his desk and looked up at Jeannie, who was watching him with fresh concern. What? he asked.

Nothing, she said.

Well you clearly ain't happy about something. He's just doing what he thinks is right.

I know, that's the problem. He should be preventing crime, not worried about upholding some damned anti-tethering ordinance. I swear, this town's going to be the death of me.

Not if Jeffrey Barber has anything to do with it. Jeannie picked up the paper and opened it and read aloud: Ineptitude. Dereliction of duty. Gross negligence.

Those are just words. Everybody's got a right to their opinion.

If that were all he wanted. She turned and walked out to her work area and she came back in carrying a sheet of paper. She handed it to him.

This came in on the fax after we talked this morning.

What's this?

Freedom of Information request, she answered.

On what?

What do you think?

Monroe reached for the glasses in his shirt pocket. What's he want?

All of it, everything. Logs. Recordings. Documents. Investigation notes. He wants everything from the moment the boy's daddy first called it in.

We've already shared with him everything we can?

I guess he's just not satisfied with that. Shame on me, I should have asked. How's your father?

He's well, Jeannie. Thank you for asking.

And his memory?

Monroe shrugged. There's good days and bad. Mostly, they tell me, he still walks around acting like he's a sheriff.

He still asking about going home?

Everyday.

The telephone rang and Monroe reached over and answered it. He sat listening.

Hmm-hm. We were just talking about it, Mr. Forster. All right. Yessir. Can I ask who gave him that idea? No, no, it's no trouble. It was just a matter of time before someone did us that little favor so it might as well been one of us. Sure thing. You have a nice day, too.

Monroe hung up the phone and sat staring down at his desk.

What is it? Jeannie asked.

He looked up at her. Trouble, that's what I'd call it.

-Evan Meade

The lights went out at the savings and loan just before noon as Evan was standing behind his desk. He was packing a few things in his briefcase and he looked up and listened and then shut the lid and walked out into the hall. Several of his co-workers were standing outside their offices looking around confused. He closed his door and walked past them and downstairs to the lobby. He stopped on his way out the building and left word with the receptionist that he'd be out for the rest of the day, then he stepped out onto the sidewalk, where across the street at the jail the jackhammer had suspiciously fallen silent.

He drove across town and into the outskirts and when he pulled into the development and onto his street he almost ran into the old lady, Mrs. Dryer, as she was crossing in front of his house. He stopped to let her pass. The redheaded woman looked shaken and all out of sorts and she averted her eyes when she saw him.

Evan parked in the garage and closed the garage door and walked out to the end of the drive. There was no sign anywhere of the woman. He walked over to the mailbox and collected the mail and he was walking back to the house when he saw the note taped to the front door. He pulled it loose and opened and read. The message was written in cursive scribble on official Homeowner's Association letterhead and simply stated that with all that was going on in their home the neighborhood thought it might require the services of a professional lawn care service. Out of consideration, the note's thoughtful sender had even stapled a business card to it.

He tucked it in with the rest of the mail and walked around the corner and inside the house where he set it aside on the counter. He opened the refrigerator and took out a can of beer and poured it into a glass and had drunk nearly half of it when Angela came in through the door.

You're home, she said.

Surprise.

She dropped her keys on the counter and noticed his glass of beer and began sorting through the mail. Kind of early for that, isn't it? she asked without looking up.

He didn't answer.

She read the note from Mrs. Dryer and laid it down and placed both hands on her hips. She looked around the kitchen.

You see the invitation? he asked.

What invitation?

The one about hiring a lawn service.

I saw it, she answered. She walked over and stood in front of the refrigerator and held the door wide open.

You think I should call them? he asked.

Yard people?

Yes.

She shrugged. I can't say I don't see their point.

Evan finished the last of his beer and put the glass in the sink and he turned and saw her looking at him. She looked at the glass. He picked it up and rinsed it out and put it in the dishwasher.

That's broken, remember?

He picked up the glass again and wasn't quite sure what to do with it so he put it back in the sink.

She slammed the refrigerator door and stepped over to the sink where she flipped on the faucet and squirted a shot of liquid detergent into a cleansing pad and started washing out the glass.

I'll do that, he said.

She acted like she hadn't heard him.

I'll do that. He nudged her to the side and reached for the glass.

Don't push.

I'm not pushing. I said I'd take care of it and I will. He took the glass from her.

Fine. She stomped back to the refrigerator.

What's got in to you?

Nothing's got into me, she insisted, then she pulled out a plastic container and opened it and stuck her nose inside it and sniffed. She made a face and closed the lid and threw the container into the garbage bin. She took out several more plastic containers and inspected their contents one at a time dropping one after another into the trash.

It looks like something's wrong, Evan said. When she didn't reply he said, I spoke to Forster today.

What about?

Evan looked at her quietly, then went on: He thinks I should hire a private investigator.

Why does he think that?

Why?

Yes, why?

To find Oliver.

Angela turned her head and scowled at him. I mean, why does he think a private investigator will have any more luck than they have had. Or haven't, I should say.

He didn't say.

She reached inside a crisper drawer and came out with a head of lettuce still wrapped in cellophane. She closed the door and went to the sink. And what did you tell him?

I didn't tell him anything.

Aren't they the ones needing help? Shouldn't they be doing the hiring?

That's not the way it works.

Well maybe it should. She pulled off a few leaves of lettuce and dropped them into a bowl and started cutting up a tomato.

Then your answer is no.

She looked at him. Are you serious?

Evan watched her and he turned and looked out the window and into the yard where two houses down a couple of teenagers were in their backyard holding on to one another. The boy had his arm around the girl's waist and they were standing and laughing and fooling around just out of reach of a dog tied up to a doghouse. The dog stood at the end of the rope at the edge of the grass barking at them. Evan had seen the girl before, sunbathing in the back yard.

Angela sat down at the table with her bowl of salad. First, you haven't asked me a question, and second, it's clear by your tone you've already made your mind up.

That's not true.

He sat down across from her. I'm asking is it something we should consider.

Where would you even find one? she asked. The phone book?

Forster gave me a name.

Of course he did.

They're in Durham.

She looked at him with a mixture of disgust and hopelessness, then she stood up and carried her half-eaten salad to the sink and dumped it down the disposal and stood slouched over the counter, her head bowed, her shoulders drooping and her hands dangling over the sink.

Evan looked out the window again. The boy and girl were gone. He looked at Angela. It's been six months, he said.

I know how long it's been, she answered dryly without looking up.

How else are we going to find her?

Angela didn't answer. He watched her where she stood, her back bowed over the sink not moving.

Did you hear me? he asked.

She turned her face and glared at him. Yes, I heard you, she said through gritted teeth. I'm always the one listening to you. The problem here is that you're not listening to yourself.

What's that mean?

Nothing, she said. It means nothing.

She turned on the faucet and rinsed the bowl.

So you think we should just give up? Move on, forget about it all.

I don't think you're even capable of forgetting about her.

Evan watched her a moment, then he looked out the window and got up to leave.

Oh, no, no sir, she said to him. She slapped the handle on the faucet shutting off the water. Don't you dare sulk away, not like I'm the bad guy.

He didn't stop and she slammed the bowl down hard into the sink where it shattered into several pieces. I said don't you fucking walk away.

Evan stopped beneath the doorway leading into the hall and stood with his back to her. He turned around.

Angela had started to cry and she wiped at her eyes, leaving behind on her cheek a smear-streak of blood from where she'd cut a finger. She saw the cut and picked up a dish towel and wiped her face with it, then wrapped the towel around her hand.

You're right, she said. I do want you to forget about her. I want more than anything for you to finally forget about her and for us to move on. With or without him.

She stood looking at him. There I said it, she said. Isn't that what you expected to hear?

Evan didn't answer.

She lifted the towel and inspected her injury and she looked back at him and sneered. But you're wrong, Mr. Mensa, smarty-pants. You don't know everything. You haven't got it all figured out. I do want him back. I want him found. I want Oliver back and I want that woman thrown into jail and I especially want this whole goddamn mess far behind us. That's all I've ever wanted.

That's what I want too.

Shut up.

She glared at him. I'll tell you what else I want. I want her out of this house, and don't pretend that she's not still a part of it, because she is and you know goddamn well that she still is. You knew she wouldn't stop. You knew she wouldn't just let go of him and yet you kept pushing, you kept making it harder and harder for her. How could you not see that? How could you not fucking see it. How could I not see it?

I didn't write the court order. I'm just following it.

She cocked her head and the way she looked at him made it seem she thought differently about that. She shook her head and looked at her injured hand and then she snatched her keys off the counter and headed toward the door to go outside.

Where are you going? he asked.

She stopped and turned and looked at him again and he saw that her eyes had lost some of their hardness and he believed her about to speak, but then she turned without a word and left him alone in the house.

-Monroe

As Monroe was walking out the door of the station with one of his deputies his mobile phone went off. He took it out of his pocket and looked at it. It's Rebecca, he said. You drive. He tossed the keys to the deputy. Monroe sat down in the passenger seat and read the message she had written him.

Everything okay? the deputy asked.

Yeah.

Ain't she in school today?

Far as I know.

How's she texting then?

Monroe didn't answer. He wrote her back. It took him a while.

Lot easier just to talk, don't you think? the deputy asked when he'd finished.

Well, Clarence, there's a lot of things would be easier without it.

Within seconds the phone beeped again and Monroe read Rebecca's reply. He wrote back and then looked up at where they were.

I wish you'd quit that, Sheriff, Clarence said. Somebody might see and think I'm chauffeuring a derelict teenager.

The phone went off again and Monroe stopped and read what it said. For crying out loud, he said. She should've let me take care of it the morning like I offered.

You must not be speaking her language.

What language is that?

Youth.

Monroe wrote her again and then put the phone back in his pocket. He looked out the window. They were almost there. After we're done, he said. I need you to swing me by the pharmacy.

What are we doing here anyway? Clarence asked as they pulled up to the house.

Just checking things out.

For no reason or did that article in this morning's paper get you thinking?

You saw that?

First thing. Jeannie showed it to me.

They parked in the drive and the two of them got out of the cruiser and walked up the sidewalk past a row of dead flowers and bare patches of dirt and brown grass and they came up the steps to the door where a foreclosure sign directed them to contact the bank.

Wonder what they'd let this go for?

Why, you in the market?

The deputy shrugged. I don't know. Might make for a good rental.

So then you got some interest in being a landlord, do you?

Not really.

All right then, let's focus, shall we.

Monroe used the key and they went inside and shut the door and stood in the entrance way looking about the living room.

Strange how she left this, isn't it? Clarence said. Like she just up and walked away.

I believe that's precisely what she did.

Monroe bent down and picked up a few pieces of mail that'd been dropped through the slit in the door and he wiped the dust off on his pants leg and glanced over it and then carried it to the kitchen and set it on the counter with the rest of the bills and letters and flyers that'd been delivered since the spring.

What'll they do with this stuff? Clarence asked. He sat down at the kitchen table testing out the sturdiness of the construction.

Auction it off, I reckon. Now you just sit tight. I'm going to take a look around.

You want I should too? the deputy asked.

Monroe glanced at him as he walked away. No, you go on and relax. You might try out that new sofa set over there. It looks like it's got your name on it.

Monroe went upstairs to the bedroom where the boy slept and he walked in and sat down on the edge of the bed and he looked around. There were posters on the wall, mostly tiny pictures of things he'd drawn. A photo of him and his mother. Another of just him alone standing out in front of some museum somewhere.

He got up and went down the hall to the mother's room and stood looking in from the doorway. He wondered what her presence might feel like in the house, in particular in that room, but he felt nothing, just emptiness. He walked over to her closet and opened the door and peered in at the clothes she'd left behind. There weren't many, a few short dresses, some sweaters, couple of pairs of pants. A row of shoes lined up neatly on the floor. He looked overhead on the shelves at the rows of blankets and boxes and plastic bags. They'd all been gone through, picked over by his folks as well as the FBI. They'd turned up nothing.

He went back downstairs and found Clarence sitting on the recliner reading a children's magazine. He hopped up when Monroe walked in.

Doing some light reading? Monroe asked.

Clarence folded the magazine in half and started to tuck it into the recliner seat cushion. I'll just put this back where I found it.

Monroe watched him as the deputy slid the magazine deep into the chair's cushion. You found that there, buried like that?

Yessir. I was just doing like you suggested, test driving a few things. That couch there's not bad. Fairly new.

Can I see it?

Clarence reached back into the chair and pulled out the magazine and he handed it to Monroe.

He put on his glasses and studied the cover and mailing label.

What is it? Clarence asked.

Monroe shook his head. Probably nothing. But I'll hold on to it just the same.

-Evan Meade

When he pulled into the office park in Durham it was just after nine in the morning. He parked in the garage and followed the directions to the fourth floor where a sign on the door directly across from the elevator read Global Investigations, Inc. He walked in. The girl looked up at him from behind the counter.

He asked to see Mr. Demski.

Your name?

He told her and while he waited he studied a large world atlas that hung on the wall of the small lobby. Colored push pins marked, he assumed, some fundamentally important aspect of their business. There were none, he also noted, protruding from anywhere in Italy.

It's astonishing where lost kids can turn up these days, a voice said behind him.

Evan turned and found himself facing a tall lean man with short cropped hair. He nodded over his shoulder at the map. Were these lost or stolen? he asked.

Some of both actually, the man said. What matters is that somebody wanted them bad enough to get them back where they legally belonged. He grinned broadly and extended his hand. Carl Demski, he said.

Can I ask how long did it take you to find them? Evan asked.

That's a good question. The answer, I'm sure, won't surprise you. It takes as much time as it takes.

Evan was already not feeling good about being there and now he let his face show it.

I apologize, Demski said. That wasn't intended to sound flippant. I hope you understand. The world is a very big place, with lots of dark corners to hide. People on the run especially can become very good at not being found.

And when you've found them, Evan asked, what then?

Well, that can go any number of ways.

What is the most likely?

The most likely? Demski considered. He looked over at the girl and then back at Evan. I'd say the mostly likely is that we take them. He motioned Evan toward the hall. Shall we?

They entered into a small, dark office and the investigator asked if he could get him something to drink. Evan didn't answer. He was reading the framed document that was hanging behind by the man's desk: Department of The Army, Silver Star. For Valor, the certificate read. He looked at the investigator.

Something to drink? Demski repeated.

Evan shook his head and the two of them sat down.

I'm glad I was able to meet with you on such short notice, Demski said. That's unusual, but we just wrapped up a contract, overseas, in Sweden. My partner's still there, in fact. Anyway, you caught us at a good time.

Evan slid a hand inside his jacket and took out a photo of Anna and he glanced at it and then lowered it to his lap and he started to look up but noticed her staring up at him and he flipped it over. When he looked up again the investigator was watching him.

Demski sat forward and rested his elbows on the desk. So, let's talk about why you're here, he said. Outside of the fact that the FBI has probably let you down and you've arrived at the conclusion that what's needed to find your child is an organic change in procedure, how did you learn about us?

From them, the FBI.

Demski cocked his head slightly and regarded that. Unusual, but not out of the question. How long have they had the case?

Six months.

A while, but not really that long. I am anxious to hear where they are in their investigation, but first, I assume you have legal custody?

Yes.

Joint or sole?

Joint, but I have primary.

Demski picked up a pen and jotted a note on a yellow legal pad. That's unusual, he said, isn't it? For a judge to award primary custody to the father. Did the mother contest?

More than once, Evan said.

Any idea why the court went against her?

Evan looked at him blankly.

I know that may seem like an unfair and sexist question, Demski added, but I'm wondering, without having read the transcript, if there were special circumstances that might help explain his, or her, reasoning.

Like what?

Like what prompted the dispute in the first place? Which one of you left the other?

She left me.

Was there someone else?

Evan didn't answer.

It'll be important, Demski said, in formulating ideas of who might have helped her.

I don't know, Evan said. Maybe.

But not that you know of?

No.

She move out or did you?

She did.

And your son?

He stayed with me.

Was there any sort of an agreement when she left concerning his custody? In other words, did the two of you have a plan on how to deal with his custody?

There was nothing in writing.

But you talked about it, you and she?

Yes, we'd talked about.

At some point then the question of custody went to the courts?

That's right.

Demski sat back in his chair. He was quiet and thoughtful. When he sat forward again he said, I'd like to see transcripts of the trial. You mentioned more than one hearing.

There was an appeal and then two others.

Demski wrote something down, then he sat back and looked across the desk at Evan. If you decide to pursue this with us, I'll want transcripts of all of the court hearings, a timeline of what happened when, lists of friends, family members, places of address, things like that.

All right.

I'll warn you it can get costly.

I understand.

You probably don't really, but we'll get to that. The investigator shifted his eyes to the picture Evan was still holding face down in his lap. May I?

Evan handed it to him.

She Latino?

Italian.

Right, you mentioned Italy when we talked on the phone. Demski turned the photo over, saw it was blank on the other side and he flipped it back around and looked at it once more. He looked at Evan. You have one of your son?

Not with me, I don't. I have them at home.

Demski handed the picture back to him. All right, he said. I've done most of the talking, but I assume you have some questions for me. Afterwards then, perhaps, we can talk about your ex-wife.

-Anna

She opened her eyes. It was night still. A sound had woken her and she lay on her side not breathing, trying to pinpoint the source.

Through her window and four floors down came the rattle of an idling engine, the clink of metal against metal, a sharp mechanical grind of a payload door sliding open. Then nothing. A few faint notes of uncertain activity.

She lay there too tired to move, just listening, wondering if the next thing she might hear was the thunderous crash through her own front door of men with guns and warrants. She wanted at least to be wearing a robe if that were the case and so she raised herself to an elbow and looked over her shoulder before slipping her legs from beneath the covers. Then she heard the dairyman's voice call out to his friend the baker and she dropped back down on the bed.

As the two men talked she listened like a beggar to the bits of their conversation. Politics. Weather. The threat of rising prices. Then again the weather. The heat had touched off nerves. The heat and so much rain. She clung tiredly to the prospect that one of them might drop some comment of value to her, a rumor or observation that might reveal some flaw to the story she'd woven of herself and Oliver. But she had been on her guard, if nothing else on her guard, and in conversations with the people she'd met in this, their new home, she had erred on the side of revealing too little. But that too could be misconstrued, as reticence raises suspicion as much if not more than braggadocio.

The two men finished their business and the deliveryman went about on his way and she closed her eyes and drifted back to asleep. When she awakened again at dawn it was from a dream in which she'd found on the walls of her old house, scribbled in crayon in a child's choppy hand, clues to their whereabouts—names, addresses, numbers—and other crude stick-figure drawings. Oliver was not with her in the dream and she had this sense that he was some place lost, but the feelings she felt toward him were of anger and in her dream she had cursed and flung threats like turds as she rushed through the house washing the walls of their filth with a dirty wet rag.

She turned to her side and looked with remorse at the boy where he lay sleeping. His cheeks were full and round, his lips were slightly parted, both of his hands were tucked beneath his head, as if in child's prayer. His skin felt cold and she reached down and gathered the sheet at his feet and fitted it around his shoulders. Oliver opened his eyes and looked at her. She smiled.

Is it raining? he asked.

No, it's not raining. She brushed back his hair. Go back to sleep.

I thought I heard thunder.

It was nothing, just a dream.

Oliver blinked and she watched as the two tiny pinpricks of glimmering light pointed at her and then closed. They opened and closed once more, the light in them like a pair of solitary lighthouses.

She slid out of the bed and went down the hall to the kitchen and flipped on the light above the sink and prepared a pot of coffee. While it brewed she went to the table and sat down. Out the window and off to the west a charcoal band of clouds hung low in the blue-gray dawn. Beneath the red, clotted rooftops the streets were quiet and dusty. Two early risers strolling along in the shadows. A pair of gypsies by their looks, in their bright colored rags to take up their ambush positions at the Duomo or the Palazzo Vecchio or Santa Croce.

She watched them until they moved out of sight then she looked out above the city, past the spires of San Lorenzo and the reserved Orsanmichele and the towering kinsman, the Badia and Bargello, and beyond the mud-colored campanile and the bell towers and the ruined city walls to where the hills of the surrounding countryside rose up like some dream in eternal defiance of all that had ever stood against them.

She closed her eyes and pictured herself just another anonymous face among the many centuries of lives that had lived there, amidst the imaginative grandeur of this living museum, of its triumphs and disasters, of its secrets. All around her in the squares and on the streets, on the crafted sandstone steps of its art and architecture there emitted from Florence an inspirational spirit of great expectation, as if it were not a question of what could happen, but more a matter of when. It suggested a feeling of infinite hope and in that regard the City of Flowers was perfect.

It was what she needed most: resilience and optimism.

At six a.m. she woke him, and again after she'd dressed. Come on, she said. We'll be late. He rolled away from her and buried his head in the pillow. Oliver, come on.

But, Mom.

No buts. She flipped the sheets to the foot of the bed and the boy scrambled around with his eyes clamped tight and he found the edge of the sheet and pulled it back around his shoulders. Remember what today is? she asked.

He didn't answer.

Remember?

Yes, I remember.

You don't sound very excited.

I am, he grumbled.

You don't sound it. She pulled his legs to the edge of the bed. Let's go. I already laid your clothes out.

She got him up and he sulked out of the room and she got herself ready and later found him sitting at the table, still dressed in his pajamas, looking out the window and eating a bowl of cereal.

Is that what you're wearing to your first day of school? she asked. She poured a cup of coffee and went and sat across from him. Hello, she said when hadn't answered.

No.

You will if you don't get dressed.

She leaned over and looked outside and saw despite the threat of rain boat crews were sculling the river. They were racing between the shallow falls and the Ponte San Niccolò, the bridge that crossed the Arno near their apartment building. They had seen them before, the rowers, their voices carrying across the stillness of morning as they built their own cadence, stretching it out like the lungarno, the river roads that lined the water's bank. Later the old fishermen would join them, rain or shine, spreading their fishing lines in the current and keeping mostly to themselves, only occasionally their voices rising against one another or the river or the fish that refused the hook. They would be there all day until darkness drove them away and even then a few remained, men like her father, or so she'd been told, their shadows pinned down in the dark, breathless, quiet, dimly illuminated by the light of a kerosene lamp as their fishing lines stretched taught between the rod and the river's current.

They ate. She glanced through yesterday's paper where on the front page was a satellite image taken of a hurricane situated off the eastern US seaboard. Red arrows indicated the hurricane's forecasted path through South Carolina and areas north. She studied the path.

How can they know that, she said and she got up and took the paper and threw it in the waste basket and walked back over to the table and sat down. Oliver was looking at her.

What? she asked.

I didn't say anything.

When they had finished eating she cleaned up the kitchen while Oliver changed into his school clothes. Did you brush your teeth? she asked when he came back into the room.

Mom?

Go.

It had started to rain and they grabbed their rain jackets and an umbrella as they left the apartment and they walked downstairs and out into the day. They hurried across the piazza and came to the newspaper stand where the shop owner greeted them.

Buon giorno, signora. He looked down at Oliver and said, Buon giorno, giovanotto.

Hi, Oliver answered.

In Italian please, Anna told him.

Buon giorno, he replied.

The newspaper vendor, whose name was Giovanni, smiled and disappeared into a small, curtain-covered storage room behind the counter. A moment later he reappeared carrying a wire rack of postcards. He came around the counter and met Oliver blocking his path. Scusi, signore, he said to him.

Anna pulled him aside and she picked up the Herald Tribune and saw it was the same as yesterday's edition.

Giovanni explained that the carrier was running behind. He offered to save her a copy when it arrived.

Grazie, she replied.

And you, signore, Giovanni said to Oliver, who was studying a colorful poster advertising some upcoming annual event. He waited for the boy to look up. Ti piace Firenze?

The boy glanced at the shopkeeper then over at his mother.

He asked if you liked it here, she told him.

Oliver shrugged and drew his face into a frown as he thought about it and said, It's okay. Then went back to reading the poster.

His mother stared blankly at him.

My boy, Giovanni interjected switching to English, you are in Florence! You must act it! He looked at Anna and pointed at the poster. You know of this? he asked. La Festa Della Rificolona?

She looked at the poster. No, she said and shook her head.

Ah, I am failing you in my job. Your uncle would not approve. You must go. This is what Florence does best. A night of lights and celebration. A night when ancient times come alive in the streets. You would love it. He looked at Oliver. You would love it, he said warmly.

Oliver looked up from the counter at them. He looked at his mother. Can I get some chocolate?

Not before school, she said.

Tore will take you, Giovanni said to her. I will speak to him.

Please don't, Giovanni, Anna told him. He has already done plenty for us.

Nonsense. He adores you. He will insist.

Anna watched him and she looked at her watch and she told Oliver they needed to go, but then she asked Giovanni if he'd heard from Alfredo.

No, he answered. You are expecting him?

She shook her head. No. I was just was wondering.

But everything is okay?

Si. Si, she said and they said their good-byes and they left and walked on beneath the umbrella and when they came to the river and the Ponte San Niccolò Oliver stopped and he asked about the boaters.

I don't know where they went, she said.

They couldn't have just disappeared.

The rain probably drove them in. She looked down at Oliver and noticed him reach into his pocket and take something out and then put it back in his pocket. What's that? she asked.

He didn't answer.

Oliver?

It's just a toy.

A toy? You brought a toy from home?

He nodded.

Why?

Just something to play with.

You're going to school, not a playground.

I won't play with it there.

Why don't you leave it with me then? She held out her hand.

He took his hand from his pocket and opened it to show it was empty. There, I put it away.

She looked at her watch. We're going to be late. Come on.

When they reached the school they stopped and stood looking up the steps at the large, grand entrance. Here we are, she said.

Oliver was following the movements of one of the nuns who was standing just outside the doorway directing traffic.

Okay? she asked.

I'm fine, Oliver replied, but she could see by the look on his face he wasn't fine.

She pointed up the steps. That's Suor Maria Grazia. You remember her. She's expecting you today. You liked her, didn't you?

I couldn't understand her.

She was speaking Italian.

Sometimes she spoke English.

Anna put her arm around him and squeezed. You're going to like it here, I promise. It's going to be so much fun and you will learn so much.

I can learn from you, you're a teacher.

I teach art.

Oliver looked back up at the nun. A tear pooled at the corner of his eye. She wiped it away. I don't want to go, he said.

Of course you do. Why not? It's school. You like school.

I like your school. I want to be with you.

She knelt in front of him and took his hand and pulled his chin to look in her eyes seriously. Oliver, we talked about this. There is nothing to worry about.

The boy didn't answer. She watched him and waited and when he finally looked at her on his own she smiled and licked her thumb and smeared away a bit of dried milk. We're together and we're okay. Right?

He nodded. She took a tissue from her purse and she used it on his cheeks and around his eyes and then she stood up straight and holding his hand started up the steps.

The nun had been watching them and she saw Oliver and her face folded into a frown. She lifted her huge arms above her head and lunged forward. No, no, no, no, no, she cried. None of that. No crying.

Oliver shied away from the large, thunderous woman. He clung to his mother's leg.

It's okay, Anna said. She detached him from her leg and brought him around. She's just going to walk you to class.

Sister Maria Grazia smiled and made a comment about his first day in school, but she said it in Italian and Oliver didn't understand and he pulled back again against his mother.

Anna glared at the nun. In English, per favore.

The nun looked shocked but said, If you wish, and she reached down and took Oliver gently by the hand and she spoke to him softly in his ear as she led him up the steps. At the top they stopped and Oliver turned and he looked at his mother and the nun spoke to him again and he lifted his hand in a halfhearted wave and Anna waved back and she forced on her face a smile, but seeing his face and knowing his fear and the hurt and the shame he was feeling, and knowing that it was all because of her and what she had done, it was all she could do not to cry out his name and run up the steps and hold him.

-Evan Meade

What makes you think he can find them? Angela asked.

They were sitting in the kitchen at their house and Evan had been watching her in the mid-morning light, reflecting on how sickly and gaunt and older she looked hunched over the table across from him. She was smoking a cigarette and her legs were crossed and she was still dressed her pajamas, an extra-large forest green tee shirt proclaiming herself in bright pink lettering Too Hot To Handle. She looked nothing of the woman he'd married.

There's nothing for sure, he answered.

She nodded as if that was just the response she'd expected of him. She took a long drag on the cigarette and leaned her head toward a crack in the window and blew a stream of gray smoke through her nose at the opening. When she finished she said, Well, one thing probably is, how much is he wanting?

Evan didn't answer and she looked at him. She drew one last time on the cigarette and slid the butt through the slit in the window and folded her arms in front of her. So is this how it's going to be?

How's what going to be?

This. Us. You're exclusion of me.

Evan didn't know what to say to her, or even what to think about it. By the time he'd gotten back from Durham and his meeting with Demski it'd been late and he'd found her lying in bed, buried beneath the covers. He'd considered waking her but thought if he reached out to touch her he'd find she wasn't even there, that the shape on her side of the bed was nothing more than a couple of pillows arranged to look like a body, like a prisoner does just prior to escape. Maybe it was better to not even know.

She picked up the crinkled pack of cigarettes and started to extract another, but instead laid it back down. She looked at him. I'm going to go visit my mother, she said.

When?

Today.

For how long?

A while.

What's a while?

I don't know, Evan. A couple of days, I guess.

He regarded her steadily.

I just need some time to myself, she said.

You won't get that at your mother's.

I won't get it here either.

They sat without talking then until Angela finally stood and went over and poured herself a cup of coffee. She dumped what was left in the pot down the drain. Evan watched her from across the small room. Despite a penchant for aerobics her night shirt hung from her shoulders like an ill-fitted pillowcase, disclosing nothing of her femaleness, nothing of a shape at all, as if her fitness goal was to whittle herself down to nothing.

So is that what you're going to do?

He looked her in the face. What?

Hire this private investigator?

He didn't answer. He looked out the window.

I don't understand why you can't at least talk to me about it.

The room grew quiet. After a moment he turned and looked at her. She was standing by the counter with her hands on her hips watching him. Well, I'll tell you what I think anyway, she said as she picked up a dish cloth from the sink and started to wash out her coffee mug. I think you should talk to someone else.

What would that do?

She stopped what she was doing and glared at him. If it was possible, her shoulders sagged even further beneath the weight of their argument, beneath the weight of his wearing her down. The blood drained from her face. She shrugged her shoulders and went back to rinsing out the coffee mug. You know what, just forget it.

She dried the cup with a dish towel and put it away in the cupboard and as she was leaving the kitchen she said, I may call you from my mother's.

Later, after she was gone, Evan drove into town and he stopped by his attorney's law office and he told him about his intent to hire a private investigator. As he spoke the attorney settled back in his chair until it was almost touching the wall. He folded his hands in front his large belly and regarded his client a moment.

You don't approve? Evan asked.

It's not that I don't approve. The attorney wiggled himself to an upright position and leaned forward on his forearms. But these kinds of, shall we say enterprises, are not usually the best use of someone's money. How much is he charging you?

Five hundred dollar retainer. The expenses go up from there. I guess it depends on where they find them.

What does the FBI say about it?

They recommended them.

The attorney sat quietly. He seemed to be deep in thought. He reached out a short, stubby arm and picked up a pencil off the desk and used it to scratch behind his ear. He said, I wish there was something more I could do. I suppose I should give this fella a call. Just let him know who I am.

He looked seriously at Evan over his glasses. My advice to you is be careful. People like this, these privatized commando-types, sometimes they're nothing more than thugs who think their occupation and license lifts them above the law. They practice the notion that the right circumstance—which is your money and a desperate situation—gives them the right to take liberties with someone else's constitutional rights.

She took my son, he said.

I know, I know, the attorney said, raising his hands defensively. I just want to caution you. Some people, and I'm not saying your guy here is one of them, but some people won't stop at anything. They'll bend every will in the way to get what they're after, especially if money's involved, and that includes yours.

I guess you get what you pay for.

Not always, Mr. Meade, and that's what I'm trying to warn you against. Money alone will not find your son. It's going to take something else and if I knew what that something was I would be in that business myself. I don't. And I doubt seriously your man here knows either. But I do know there are laws protecting people, all people, including your ex-wife, and those laws can't be broken, not even at the sake of righting a serious wrong.

Evan considered that. You think I'm wasting my money then?

The attorney stood up. His time for dolling out free advice was over. Well, sir, that's the beauty of a free market. It's your money to spend in whatever way you deem necessary.

-Monroe

When Monroe pulled into the construction zone there was one of his trucks in the parking lot but the contractor wasn't anywhere to be found. He had waited ten minutes when two men came out of the building carrying their coolers and they looked at him and climbed in the cab of the truck and then drove off. Monroe was about to do the same when another white truck pulled up.

Sorry, Sheriff, the contractor said as he stepped out of his vehicle.

I hope it was nothing too serious.

You been inside?

No, I've been sitting here waiting on you.

You could've gone in at least, looked around. Someone should've seen to that.

I believe that's your job, Danny.

They commenced on his walkthrough and once they were finished Monroe had a few questions about the armory and security and then he asked how much longer it'd be before they turned over the keys.

Difficult to say, Sheriff. Most of the heavy work's done. As you just saw, we got a little bit of work in the offices still to do, around the holding area. Some tidying up here and there.

That's not exactly an answer.

A month, maybe two.

That's what you said back in July.

Well, Sheriff, he said We've been competing against other things.

Like cut power lines.

I was talking mostly about the weather, but yes that too, and also there's the normal red tape to contend with. Don't forget about that.

You're reminding me of it right now.

From the jail Monroe walked across the street and down a short ways to the main branch of the city library and he went inside. He saw the librarian was helping twin girls and their mother check out. He walked up to the counter. Afternoon, Mrs. Jennings. Girls. The twins looked at him and said hello. Sheriff, their mother replied. He looked at the woman helping them. Ms. Grace, he said.

The librarian leered at him, Hello yourself, Mr. Sheriff. To what do we owe this honor?

Just in the neighborhood, he said. Thought I'd stop by.

She looked at him doubtfully and went back to scanning the books. Monroe glanced down at the two little girls, who hadn't taken their eyes off him. He bent down. How are you two? he asked them.

Fine, they answered.

You both coming later this week to our parking lot party?

The twins stared blankly at him and then turned their heads up to look at their mother. Of course, she replied. We wouldn't miss it, Sheriff.

He nodded. You won't regret it, he said to the girls. I promise. They'll be rides, food, special prizes.

You remember last year, their mother said. You both got fingerprinted.

The twins nodded.

Well, then good, he said. I'll see you both there then.

The girls nodded and after they left it was just him and the librarian. I assume those airmen will be there again this year.

They're aviators, not airmen, he told her.

Whatever. Those pretty boys in their jump suits.

She took off her glasses and left them dangling from a small chain where they laid against her chest and she looked at Monroe and saw he was watching there too and she smiled with amusement. He blushed and looked away and she pushed her flaming red hair from out of her face and gathered a stack of books in her arms to carry. She said to him, You think boys are the only ones allowed to look?

Here, let me get that, he said and he came around the counter and took them from her. Where to?

She pointed toward her office. Where have you been anyway? If I didn't know any better. I'd think you were trying to avoid me.

I'm here now, aren't I?

But I'm not the reason why.

How do you know that?

A woman just knows.

She showed him where to put them and he set them down.

As matter of fact, he said, I need your help.

What kind of help?

The solving crime kind.

Oh, my favorite, she said sarcastically, then she tossed her hair back and sat down. She crossed her legs. Let's hear it then.

He handed her the magazine he'd taken from the Anna Miller's house.

What's this?

I'm hoping it's something I haven't seen in my job for what feels like a very long time.

What's that?

Opportunity.

-Anna

She stood at the blackboard having just lectured to the classroom of students on the use of light and shadow and as she was giving them their instructions a girl in the front row raised her hand.

Sì, Sofia? Anna said.

Pensavo che dovevamo dipingere, the girl said. She looked around to see if the others agreed and several were shaking their heads. One boy in the back mumbled something and a couple of the children sitting closest to him snickered.

Silenzio, Anna told them. She looked at the girl. Questo e la classe di arte.

Dipingere è arte.

Sò bene. Anna waited for the girl to agree. When she did not she looked out at the rest of the class. Per favore classe, se lei—

The girl Sofia interrupted to repeat once more that they were told there would be painting in this art class.

Anna offered her a reassuring smile. Ti prometto che dipingeremo eventualmente.

The girl was about to argue further when there came a knock at the door. Anna walked over and opened the door partway and saw Oliver standing in the hall, his eyes were pointed down toward the floor and standing behind him with his hands on the boy's shoulders was her principal, Nicola Bonelli.

She pushed open the door and Oliver, with his head still lowered, suddenly lurched into her legs. She looked at the top of his head and then at the principal. Cosa c'è? she asked.

Good Morning, Signora, the principal answered in English. I apologize for the interruption. He gazed down at Oliver, who had his face buried in the folds of her skirt. It seems your son ran away from school.

Ran away? She pried his arms from around her and held him at arm's length. You ran away from school?

Oliver didn't answer.

Answer me.

Yes.

Why? Where were you going to go?

He shrugged.

Do you know your way around? Do you know anyone who could even help you find your way around?

No.

Then why on earth did you run away?

Oliver stared quietly at the floor. The principal cleared his throat. She looked at him. Perhaps we should talk alone, he said. Just the two of us.

She led Oliver by the hand to her desk and made him sit down. Do not under any circumstance get up. Do you understand?

She ordered the class to get started with their work and then she stepped out into the hall where the principal stood waiting. Dove l'ha trovato? she asked.

One of the nuns from San Michele brought him to me.

Perché?

Prego?

Why didn't they just take him back to his classroom?

He shrugged I'm afraid I don't know.

Well they shouldn't have brought him here. She turned and looked through the glass at Oliver. He'll get the wrong message.

She turned back toward the principal. I'm sorry for the disruption, she said. I assure you it won't happen again.

The principal nodded. He motioned her toward an empty classroom across the hall. Would you mind?

It dawned on her then he was still speaking to her in English. She pointed over her shoulder at her door. Devo occuparmi della mia classe.

He smiled. Por favore, he said Un momento.

They sat down at a pair of students' desks across the aisle from one another. The principal watched her. We've not had much opportunity to talk, he said, you and I. I trust you have everything you need.

Yes, I think so.

And the staff, the other teachers, you've found them to your liking?

Yes, of course. They've all been very kind.

Bene, Bene, he said, then fell quiet a moment. He reached into his shirt pocket and took out a pack of cigarettes and tapped the pack against his palm and he pushed one up from the bottom and took it and offered the pack to her. She shook her head and he stuffed the cigarettes back into his pocket and got up from the chair and walked to the front of the classroom where he picked up the teacher's wastebasket and carried it back to the desk. He produced a lighter from his pocket and sat down.

This is your son's first year of school? he asked.

Yes, it is.

You chose not to put him in the international school?

That's right.

May I ask why?

Well, she said. It is very competitive, and San Michele is closer and it too is a very good school.

But he struggles with the language, no?

Yes, she agreed. For now he does. But he's getting better.

He nodded.

She watched him smoking and wanted to get back to her classroom.

He flicked the cigarette toward the waste basket spilling most of the ashes on the floor and said to her, I understand that at San Michele it is also very difficult school to gain admission, especially if you are not from here.

She did not say anything back to him and he watched her and he drew on the cigarette and held the smoke a moment and closed his eyes and exhaled and when he opened them he leaned back in his chair and looked about the room and he looked at her.

You seem like an intelligent woman, he said. Had I been involved in your hiring I might have found you something better than teaching art to seventh graders.

I like what I do.

Sciocchezze! He waved his hand and sent ashes spilling toward the floor. Children this age are crazy and clueless with hormones! But I am more interested in you.

He leaned forward and rested one hand on his knee. You see, this is what I can't quite figure. You are not from Florence. You have a child that speaks only English, who attends a very expensive and exclusive school, and yet you live without a husband or additional source of income.

He sat back and shook his head and regarded her with puzzlement. You understand, don't you, how I might be puzzled by that?

Anna looked at him and she looked down at her lap. She curled one hand into the other. Across the hall she could hear the sound of the children in her classroom growing louder. I'm not sure I understand the question, she said.

The principal watched her. He turned the cigarette in his hand and extinguished it on the underside of the desktop and then stood up. Perhaps it is a discussion for another time, he said to her. After all, your students await you.

She went ahead of him into the hall.

He is a very smart boy, the principal said behind her. Your son. We had a very interesting conversation.

Anna stopped at the door to her classroom. She thanked him for bringing this to her attention and she opened the door and went in and closed it. The students fell immediately quiet. She walked up to her desk and told Oliver to take a seat at one of the empty chairs along the back wall.

He looked at her.

Go on.

He stood with his arms hanging limp by his side and slunk back to the desk and sat down. He laid his head on the table. Outside in the hall, through the tiny window glass the principal stood there still watching.

                                                    -Evan Meade

He came dragging out of the garage, dripping with sweat.
He was done with it for now. His arms and pant legs and
torso were flecked with the chewed up scraps of grass,
leaves and dark shrubbery and in the air all about the dirt
and detritus that his mowing had stirred up hung in the
stillness like some befouled contaminate on the rays of
morning sunlight that broke through the gaps in the trees.

He came around to the back of the house and pulled one
of the patio chairs to the edge of the slab and he peeled off
his tee shirt and used it to wipe away the yard trimmings
from his forearms and then he sat down. He took off his
shoes and socks and brushed the debris from his pants legs
and stretched his legs out and leaned back and sat there
looking out on the day as if someone, a neighborhood spy
perhaps, or even Mrs. Dryer herself, were secretly watching
and would take chagrined note of how shrewdly he'd
handled the lawncare matter.

Inside the house the phone rang. He scratched at his
forearms and listened for the machine to pick up but
whoever it was had hung up as the house fell back to quiet.
After a while he got up and walked inside and over to the
answering machine and confirmed there was no message
waiting for him and he picked up the phone and called his

office and left word that he would not be in today. He went to the kitchen and drew a glass of water from the sink and was looking out the window at the house next door when the door opened and the woman came out carrying the little girl in her arms. He watched her as she belted the child in her car seat and she walked around the front of the vehicle and looked over and shook her head at his morning's handiwork. He smirked as he set down the glass in the sink.

Later, after he'd showered, he stood looking up at the ceiling in the hall where he'd just lowered the attic door. Particles of dust and insulation drifting to the floor. Him gazing up into the darkness.

The phone rang again but he ignored it and started up the wooden ladder. He stopped near the top and felt in the dark for the string and found it and gave it a tug. Then he came up the rest of the way. He stood looking around at the general condition: pockets of insulation, scattered mouse turds, large plastic totes of decorations, bags of old clothes, an odd assortment of cardboard boxes, a loosely stacked piled of unused picture frames.

He stepped over the frames and walked back to the corner of the attic where they kept the pieces of luggage and empty product boxes and he pulled out a small cardboard box from near the bottom of the stack and carried it back to the opening in the floor. He set the box down and looked it over. It looked to him undisturbed and he gathered it up and backed carefully down the steps. He set it down in the middle of the living room floor, then went and got a paring knife and slid it along the edges and peeling back the flaps looked inside.

On top was a photo of Anna. It was taken during their first winter in the house. She was standing outside next to the boxwoods he had just that morning butchered with the grass trimmer, but at the time the picture was taken were then covered with several inches of snow. She was four or five months pregnant, smiling broadly and her belly just starting to show.

He laid the photograph aside and dredged several more from the box, looking at them one by one, pausing only rarely to reminisce, mostly just looking to see if there was some change of expression in them, some glint of the treason to come. He set the photos aside and dug through the rest of the contents until he found the things he'd been thinking of since the day before: a thick manilla folder of official documents, the divorce decree, court transcripts and such. The things Demski had asked him about.

He took the folder from the box and leafed through it. When he came across a standard sized white envelope he held it up to the light and he looked at it and could see the feint outline of the letter inside. He set it aside and he glanced through the rest of the folder's contents then he closed it and set the folder to the side as well and he reached back into the box and felt with his hands toward the bottom for the stiff cardboard protectors.

Pinched between them was an 8 x 10 portrait of Anna she'd sketched in pencil. In it she was standing before a full length oval mirror and dressed only in a wedding veil, white panties and garter belt. Her right hand covered her breasts and her position in the mirror provided only a shadowy glimpse of her inner thighs. The drawing had been meant as a joke, but showed just enough indelicacy in Anna to galvanize his heart rate, even now, after all she'd done to him. The script in the lower right hand corner read, On My Wedding Day.

He stared at the sketch until he felt his mouth had gone dry and he put it back down in the box and he closed the panels and rose and went to the kitchen and opened a bottle of beer and he carried it back to the living room and stood looking out the sliding glass door at the world.

This is how you woo me back? she said from across from their kitchen table. One of their final nights together. With some letter?

He didn't answer, but sat staring down at the table.

You don't even mean these things you wrote in here. She tossed the envelope between them. He looked at at it, then at her. I used to pretend that you did, she said, but I was wrong.

Evan looked away.

I wonder, she said, does this even bother you?

Does what?

This, what Oliver is going through? She started to cry.

Does it bother me?

Yes.

I didn't cause it, he answered.

All I ever wanted was a family.

Evan looked down at his hands. I would've given you that.

When? She smacked her fist down on the table, tears now streaming. With this? she waved her hand in an arc. With this house I never wanted? With Oliver staying in daycare because you didn't want me to stay home? When, Evan? When? When exactly were you thinking of giving me that?

He looked at her and said nothing, letting his silence wear her down.

I can't leave him, she finally, shaking her head. She wiped at her eyes. I can't. I won't.

You mean Oliver? he asked.

Yes, of course, I mean Oliver.

He watched her. We talked about this already.

I can't, she said. I just can't.

You could stay.

She looked at him as she stood up from the table. When I go, she said, I'm taking him with me.

You can't, he said. We agreed.

Evan, I have to.

I'll stop you, he said, and he had.

-Anna

There was still a little daylight left after she'd put Oliver early to bed so she sat at the table with her sketch book open applying the finishing touches to a sketch of the view outside her window. The light hitting the skyline was not right though, barely more than a flimsy gray sheen, with no shadows, no hard lines, no heart from which all artwork arose.

After dismissing the children at the end of the school day when the final bell had sounded, she'd gone back to speak to Oliver about his running away. She had stood then looking down at the desk where he sat with his head down on top of some papers she'd given him to practice his handwriting. She'd thought him sleeping and brushed the side of his head gently with her hand.

He opened his eyes. It's time to go, she said.

He looked at her and sat up.

Gather your things.

He did as she asked. Before they left, she said to him: We need to talk about why you ran away. I just need to understand. Oliver look at me.

He did.

You could've gotten lost, or hurt. What would you have done then?

He appeared to think about it, then shrugged.

What if someone had taken you?

She perceived a slight shake of his head from him.

You just can't run away from school. You have to promise me you won't do that again. It's dangerous.

He nodded.

Promise me.

I promise.

She watched him and helped him into his backpack and as they were leaving the school she asked about his conversation with the principal. What did you talk about? she asked.

I don't know, nothing.

Well, you must've talked about something.

He wanted to know about my dad.

What did you tell him?

I told him he didn't live with us.

What did he say to that?

Nothing.

What else?

Can we get something to eat? he said.

Don't you have a snack left in your lunch bag? I packed you an extra one.

I threw it away.

What?

I threw my lunch away, too.

She stopped and looked at him. Why on earth did you do that?

He didn't answer. They started walking again.

What else did you talk about?

I can't really remember.

She walked without speaking for a moment, thinking to herself. Well did he ask about where you'd come from?

Yes.

What did you say?

I said America.

Did he ask where in America?

No.

What about your name?

My name?

Yes. Did he ask you about it? Sometimes they like to know if it's different.

He didn't ask.

But if people do, at your school or anywhere else, you know which one to use, right?

Caruso?

That's right.

I know.

She stopped and stepped in front of him to face her. Listen, she said, I know this hasn't been easy for you. I know there have been lots of changes, things happening that you might not fully understand. But—

But at least we are together, he said.

Yes. We are together, and if we want it to stay that way we have to do some things that are different. Smart things.

Like using my new last name when someone asks.

She watched him and nodded. You know how much I love you? she said. She took him by the hand and they started on again.

Oliver Caruso, she sang. It has a nice ring, don't you think?

Oliver didn't answer.

She glanced down at him and squeezed his hand. Don't you?

I liked it the way it was, he said.

She rose from the table and went to the sink and filled a pitcher and watered the herbs on the windowsill and went down the hall to the bathroom and shut the door behind her. She left the lights off and stood in the windowlight looking at her silhouette in the mirror. She slipped out of her clothes and turned slowly and she watched her reflection move in the frosted window as some brazen voyeur might: the slope of her shoulders, the poetic invitation of curves, patches of light and dark.

She turned on the shower and stepped beneath it. The water was hot and pelted her skin and she closed her eyes and turned her face toward the spray. It had been one of his favorite places to have sex, the shower. Evan. The small space, the confinement, the inability for escape. It all had made perfect sense. He'd surprise her, smiling, making a grand entrance, hard, naked, and ready to go, as if he were some kind of treat.

She had rarely resisted his come ons, though the position it required they take was uncomfortable as the shower controls pressed against her back leaving harsh indentations and the direction and misplaced intensity of his thrusts left her feeling sore and while it never lasted for long, it managed to add a few minutes of utter disruption that seemed to carry into the rest of the day. Like the deepest, most long lasting regret.

Monroe sat listening from his front row seat at the commissioner's meeting as the lady, Betsy Bible, from the Humane Society spoke. We have an ordinance in this county that protects animals, she was saying. It's a good ordinance. It's fair and plainly written. Everyone understands it. The problem is our sheriff's department is simply not enforcing it and these animals are paying a horrific, deadly price for their shameless disregard.

An angry voice from the back of the council room called for her to mind her own business.

Monroe turned as did all eyes on the perpetrator who was even then in the process of being escorted from the room with his arms pinned to his sides by one of his deputies.

A murmur rolled through the crowd.

The Chair banged her gavel.

The lady turned back to the bench and continued, It's precisely this kind of attitude that we find not acceptable. We will not mind our own business and stand by and be silent while the inhumane treatment of animals in this county continues.

One of the commissioners spoke up: What of the arrest last month, he said. We seized what, Sheriff, two donkeys, a horse and one goat.

There's no question progress has been made, the woman agreed. But there's still room for improvement. Just in that matter alone, no less than a half dozen complaints were reported to authorities in the past year about the poor living conditions of those animals. Our problem is why something was not done sooner.

What is your proposal, Ms. Bible?

For starters, we need better communication. There's plenty of room for the two organizations to work together to solve the problem. It's just not happening. For this reason, we're asking Sheriff Rossi to form a joint committee comprised of deputies and local animal rescue groups to save these neglected and abused animals of our county.

She asked did the board have any questions and when no one spoke up she thanked them for their time and sat down.

The Chair called for the sheriff to speak.

Monroe stood and stepped up to the microphone. He looked at the commissioners. He looked at Ms. Bible. In the back of the room on the last row sat the reporter Jeffrey Barber and he looked at him too before turning back to the front of the meeting hall. I'll be brief, he said. First, to address the accusation that my officers failed to respond promptly and professionally to every one of those calls made on that home, I am happy to provide a detailed account if anyone wishes. You will find that not once did my department drop the ball or otherwise acted derelict in their duties to uphold the law. We checked on those animals. Second, as everyone here knows, some amendments to the ordinance were added last year after what was a hotly contested debate. Because of the public's reaction this commission decided on and approved the establishment of an education campaign and grace period for county residents to comply.

We can educate until it's absurd. The problem has not gone away, Ms. Bible announced.

That doesn't change the law or the decisions of this commission. The arrest in this matter happened precisely when and how it should have. My officers behaved properly.

It's too little, too late, Sheriff. Much like the other actions of your department.

Another moan arose from the onlookers and the Chair again sounded her gavel.

Monroe looked back at the Board. Gentlemen, Madam Chair, attacks such as this are completely unfounded and as such I formally turn down Ms. Bible's request to form a super committee to study the problem. I'll be happy to meet with national representatives of the Humane Society to resolve their concerns, but I'll not stand by and allow somebody to insult me or any of the 170 people who work for me and whose reputations are at stake. That is all I have to say.

Monroe stepped away from the microphone and walked out of the room. The reporter Barber stood as he was leaving and followed him into the hall.

Just a word, Sheriff.

I've said about all the words I can stand for one day, Mr. Barber.

I was hoping you'd comment on those two missing persons.

You mean the whereabouts of your FOIA request?

You no doubt know the boy's father is hiring a private investigator.

So I've heard.

How do you think that reflects on you?

Monroe stopped and turned and faced him. On me?

On your handling of it.

How do you think it reflects?

The reporter looked at him. Poorly?

Monroe studied him. Stick to writing your stories, Mr. Barber. Leave the analyzing to someone else.

He left the building and walked out into the evening and down the street to the annex. He walked inside and found Stokes calling for him on the radio.

What is it? Monroe asked.

Sorry, Sheriff, he said. I wasn't sure you were coming back here. There's someone here to see you.

Monroe looked behind him at what served as a small waiting area and he saw a man sitting on a chair flipping through some brochure. By the short military haircut, pressed slacks, shined loafers and dark colored polo shirt, he knew before Stokes could even mention the stranger's name, precisely who it was.

-Evan Meade

There was one last thing, he thought, as he stood at the edge of the beam from the flood lights looking out at the vegetable garden. The decrepit untended stalks, split and broken-over, their once productive branches now spindly and brown and infested with pests and spiders. The garden's original intent now lost as the bed appeared to be gathering en masse to set ruin upon its orderly creation and fixed itself wholly on broadening its borders. Looking at it there seemed no good way to attack it, no sure fell swoop to knock it over.

He jerked the lawnmower's starter cord and unleashed the blade squarely upon it, cutting a swath down the center of it, dividing the claim of its territory. Thus, he engaged it in small sections. Even then the mowing was difficult, the tall weeds and stems bogging down the blade, the motor churning and coughing. More than once the engine died on him and he had to clear the blade of debris and restart his destructive foray.

Once he'd finished he dragged the stems and the stalks and the leftover remains and piled them in the middle of the yard, then went and got a lighter and the can of gasoline from the garage and pulled a lawn chair over and lit the pile of garden debris and sat and watched it burn. A slight satisfactory breeze carried the smoke through the dark in the direction of the Dryer home.

He was sitting there still when thirty minutes later the phone rang. He got up and answered it. It was Angela.

How's your mother? he asked.

She's fine.

When are you coming home?

I don't know. Probably not until Tuesday.

Why Tuesday?

It's just the day I'll probably come back.

It's too quiet here, he said.

Angela didn't answer.

Did you hear me?

Yes.

They were both silent then for a long while. Evan walked out and sat back down in the lawn chair to watch the fire smolder.

We need to talk about Oliver, she said. When Evan didn't respond she said, And also about her.

Her who?

His mother. Are you listening?

I'm listening.

Well aren't you going to say something?

Like what?

About us talking?

What do you want to talk about?

I just told you. About everything.

Sure, we can talk about everything, just as soon as you come home.

Why are you doing this?

Doing what?

Treating me like that, like it's somehow all my fault.

I didn't say that.

You didn't have to.

I'm not the one who bailed.

Stop it, Evan! Will you please just stop it! She sighed. I didn't bail and I don't want an argument. I just want you to talk to me.

I am, he said.

No, you're not. It's just like that thing with the private investigator. You never even gave me a chance.

That's not true.

It is true. You only asked what I thought because you were worried it would look bad if you didn't.

Evan dropped the phone to his lap. He laid his head back on the lawn chair and stared at the dying flames. When he brought it back to his ear he asked was there anything else.

Angela sighed and said that there wasn't. I'll probably be home on Tuesday, she said. Or Wednesday. I'm not sure which. When I get there I want to talk about this. Okay?

All right, he answered.

After a moment she asked, So, what else is going on?

Nothing, he said. There's nothing else going on.

-Monroe

Monroe shut the door to his office behind him. The private investigator sat down and snapped open his briefcase on his lap. He took out a file with the word MEADE written in large block letters across the tab. Monroe sat watching him from across his desk, he leaned back in his chair. When the man looked, Monroe asked, So, what can I do for you, Mr. Demski?

Well, Sheriff, as you may have heard, my firm has been hired by Evan Meade to locate his ex-wife.

You mean to say his son?

Yes, of course. It's his son who is missing. I don't mean this to come off sounding glib, but it's been my experience if you find the kidnapper you generally find the thing that was kidnapped.

Go on.

I understand the sheriff's office handled the initial investigation.

Which has been turned over to the FBI.

Who apparently recommended us to Mr. Meade.

Us?

My partner and I. He's currently on another assignment in Europe.

Which is why, I suppose, you've got an itch to get working on this one. You're hoping he's close enough to snatch this one.

Demski didn't respond right away. He looked at the sheriff and then he looked down at the file in his lap. When he looked up again at Monroe there was something wooden about him that Monroe couldn't quite put his fingers on. An hardening of his neutrality.

We help relocate and reunite people, he said.

It's not so much the outcome that has me worried as it is the tactics.

What you're thinking of are last effort scenarios. Our preference is to work with the local authorities in retrieving those individuals taken unlawfully against their consent.

Not against, but without. You mean to say without their consent. There's a difference, you know. I don't know what the father has shared with you, but there's been nothing to suggest that the boy didn't want to go with her.

Does that matter?

Monroe didn't answer right away. What matters, in my opinion, is not making things worse than they already are.

Demski didn't say anything.

With that said, Monroe said. He sat forward. The fact that the FBI is trying even to outsource this case shows you just what state it is in.

Demski nodded. I'm hoping with your help and our resources we can change that.

Monroe sat watching him. He looked at his watch. What kind of help did you have in mind?

The investigator opened his folder and took out a yellow pad of paper. I was thinking we'd start at the present and work backwards.

You mean with where they are now?

Yes sir.

Well, assuming the father's telling the truth, they could be just about anywhere.

I get this feeling you might think there's reason not to believe him?

I don't know, Mr. Demski, but I do know people and people who are involved in custody disputes tend to see what they want to see and hear what they want to hear.

But you can't dispute the fact that she took him.

She had every right to take him. She's the child's mother and it was her weekend with the boy. The problem started when she didn't bring him back.

Demski appeared to consider that. Do you have a theory on why?

Mr. Demski, Monroe said, I understand you've got a job to do and you've been paid good money to do it, but can I ask what you did before this?

I was in the Army Special Forces.

I can see that. Well, it goes without saying, I applaud both your service and your sense of law and liability, but to you and the others of us in this business we might never understand why a person does what they do. Maybe she's crazy. Maybe she just couldn't stand the thought of being without her son, or that there just wasn't any other choice than to not give him back.

And risk going to jail?

That's what I'm trying to tell you. The law itself doesn't keep people from doing bad things. It's the fear of getting caught, or as you put it, the risk of going to jail. In most cases there's nothing especially remarkable about people who break the law. Take this boy's mother for instance. She's probably not very different from any other law abiding citizen you might run into. She works to provide for herself and her son. She pays her taxes. She's a vital part of the community. In fact, the only real difference between her and anyone else is where one has hope the other has none and filling that hole is something called desperation.

Demski sat quietly looking across the table at him.

At least that's been my experience, Monroe added.

I've seen some that might surprise you.

I don't doubt that.

I don't mean that as an insult.

I didn't take it as such.

The investigator looked down at his notes. He looked at the sheriff. The FBI thinks they left the country and are somewhere in Europe.

Monroe nodded. That appears to be the consensus.

Have you've spoken with the woman's mother?

A number of times.

Mr. Meade mentioned a town in the northern part of Italy. Demski referred again to his notes. San Salvatore, he said. His ex-wife apparently lived there before her parents divorced, then moved to Naples.

You keep calling her that.

Demski looked at him.

His ex-wife. You keep calling her his ex-wife.

That's what she is.

I know that.

You prefer I refer to her as something else?

Monroe thought about it some and moved on. You're wanting to ask about her father next.

As a matter of fact, there's no record of anyone having spoken with him, biological or step either one.

One's dead and the other nobody could find. We're not even sure of his full name.

You're speaking of her birth father?

That's correct.

Is there any other family that you know of?

Not that you don't already probably know about. Grandmothers, uncles, that sort of thing.

Demski closed his file and placed it back in the briefcase. I also find it surprising that there is so little in terms of official documentation regarding Ms. Miller's U.S. citizenship. At least in terms of what Mr. Meade could provide.

I would agree with that.

My office has gone ahead and requested INS forms, birth certificate, adoption paperwork, things of that nature to attest to her U.S. citizenship. I also have a contact in the State Department who I'm hoping can help.

Well, Monroe said and he stood and came around the desk, Good luck that with that, Mr. Demski. Perhaps something will turn up.

He walked him to the door where Demski turned and faced Monroe. There is one last thing, Sheriff. I wondered if you would permit me to take a look at the house?

Sorry, I can't allow that.

Demski nodded. I understand. Well, I appreciate your time, Sheriff. Thank you for speaking with me on such short notice.

Monroe walked him outside and the two men stood at the entrance looking out on into the darkness and the empty downtown street. Monroe handed the private investigator his card. I don't mind helping, but I'll ask you to keep in mind, Mr. Demski, my first duty is to the people of this county.

Don't worry about that, Sheriff, the investigator said as he started down the steps. We're very good at what we do. They wont even know we're here.

That's precisely what I'm afraid of, Monroe said after he'd gone out of earshot.

-Anna

They'd been waiting at the bus stop for a few minutes when Anna overheard a young woman passing by say that the transportation workers had gone on strike overnight and the buses were not running from the hours of nine to noon.

She looked at Oliver. We're going to have to walk.

Why?

Because there's no one to drive the bus.

What bus?

Exactly.

She shifted her bags into one hand and took Oliver's hand by the other and led him across the street and onto the bridge where alongside the river an old man sat crouched in front of a campfire. He was sifting through the ashes with a stick while the thin line of white-gray smoke ascended like feathery tendrils around him. Behind him stood a small yellow tent.

Does he sleep there? Oliver asked.

I don't know, she said. It looks like he might.

They left the bridge and the river with the lone fisherman behind them and they came into the old city. They crossed the street and turned the corner at the Biblioteca Nazionale and entered the Piazza Santa Croce, where already there was the scent of wood glue in the air as a tourist group of fifteen or twenty early risers had surrounded one of the artisans working outside his shop door. The noisy clang of hammered wrought iron fractured the still morning air. They went on. Both were already tired and Oliver was complaining about it by the time they arrived at the Piazza Lorenzo Ghiberti.

We're almost there, she said.

Oliver's head hung low. Where are we going anyway?

To the market, she said. It's Saturday, remember?

He looked at the bags she was carrying. Are we staying again? he complained.

Just for a while.

The market was busy with people standing and milling about everywhere, spilling out onto the street, congregating around the booths, in the aisles and at the various vendor carts and wagons. Getting through the crowd was painfully slow. At one point Oliver stopped and pointed toward an old woman walking past, her arms laden with bunches of grapes and he asked, Can we get some of those?

When we come to them, she told him.

A few minutes later they finally arrived at a table where there sat a young redheaded man alone and concentrating intently over a canvas and palette of paint.

Buon giorno, Tore, she said to him.

The young man looked up from his work. He smiled at her. Ah, Anna. Buon giorno, buon giorno! Vieni, siediti.

She slid her bags under the table and flung herself down in the chair. She looked straight ahead while she caught her breath and then she turned and looked at him. A loose strand of hair had fallen into her face and she pushed it away. That's a long walk, she said.

You walked?

The buses are on strike.

He nodded. I didn't realize.

She looked at his work. It was an oil painting of a little dark-haired girl in a white dress standing before a fountain. It's beautiful, she said.

She reached down and unpacked her bags of the work she had brought and arranged them on the table. The sketch of the Florence skyline she set on a small pedestal near the corner. She sat back and studied the crowd. How is business? she asked Tore.

Scuzi?

Scusami, she said, di parlare in Inglese.

Non è ninente, he told her. It gives me a chance to work on my English. He looked up at the crowd. Besides, the tourists are more willing to talk if they know you speak their language. Today, though, they mostly seemed interested only in fresh food.

Anna turned and looked at Oliver. Here, honey, she said and she stood and took a small blanket from one of the bags and spread it out on the ground directly behind the table for him to sit on. She handed him a box of crayons and a coloring book. Okay? she asked.

He nodded.

That was a long walk. Do you need something to drink? she said.

I thought we were getting some grapes.

She sighed. She looked over her shoulder at where the grape vendor was on the other side of the crowded market, back near the main entrance. She looked at Tore and asked if he would like something and when he said that he didn't she turned to Oliver and told him to come with her.

He looked up from his coloring book. To where? he asked.

To get some grapes.

Do I have to?

You do if you want some grapes.

But, Mom.

He's fine, Tore said. I'll look out for him.

But don't you want to pick them out?

Not really.

He can color here, Tore said and they both looked over and watched as he pushed some things aside and made room for Oliver to sit beside him at the table. Who knows, he said, he might attract some customers.

Anna looked back at the market and then at Oliver, who had already climbed into the chair next to Tore and resumed coloring. Last chance, she said to him.

He acted like he didn't hear her and so she turned and threaded her way back through the throngs of people until she reached the line for the grapes. The line was long and disorderly and she had to wait a long time before it was her turn. She picked a bundle of nice looking ones and handed them to the merchant, who weighed them and told her how much she owed and she paid him and turned to go but the crowd had closed in around her and her going was slow and made more frustrating by the fact that it blocked her view of the booth where she'd left Oliver. She was slowly pushing her way through the shoppers when she bumped into a couple of young Americans asking an older woman for directions. Excuse me, she said to them and tried to step past.

Can you help us? one of the girls asked.

Anna looked at her and she looked at the other and then at the local woman, who it was clear by the blank stare on her face that she'd understood nothing of what the two girls had asked her.

We're looking for the theater della, one of the girls said and then stopped and peeked over her friend's shoulder and referred to a tour guide book. Pergola, she finished with a smile.

Anna tried to glance past them in the direction of the booth but could see nothing beyond the crowd of shoppers. She looked back at the girls. May I? she asked the one holding the guide. She studied the guide book. It's that way, she said and she pointed with her finger. Then she showed them on the map where they were versus where they wanted to be.

They thanked her and wanted to talk some more but Anna said she had to go and she left them and hurried as best as she could back to Tore's booth. When she arrived, she found Oliver gone.

Where's Oliver? she asked Tore, who was standing beside the table talking to a young couple. She peered over at the blanket. The crayons and coloring book were there where he'd left them but her son was nowhere in sight.

Tore, she said louder. He looked her way. She held up her hands. Where's Oliver?

He turned then and looked at the table where Oliver had been sitting. He looked at the blanket, then at Anna, his face expressionless.

Oliver, Anna called and she cupped her hands and called again as she looked out over the market.

He was just here, said Tore. He approached her and softly touched her shoulder. He looked out at the market. He's probably just off with a friend.

Anna jerked away. No, she said. He's not just off with a friend. He doesn't have any friends.

But he was just here, he repeated.

Anna climbed on a chair and stood looking over the heads of the crowd. She spotted near the entrance two carabinieri standing and talking to the same pair of teenage girls she'd given directions to and she thought of waving them down and asking one of the officers for help, but when one turned and looked her way his eyes narrowed at her with suspicion and she quickly stepped down from the chair. She looked at Tore.

Why weren't you watching him? she said.

Tore stared back at her. He looked caught between an apology and some useless excuse.

Oliver! Anna called.

There, Tore said and she was about to lash out at him again and yell at him for not taking her seriously when he pointed behind her. She turned to look and saw Oliver standing with another little boy a few meters away on the far side of the booth.

She came quickly around the table and stooped down in front of him and took his shoulders in both of her hands. What are you doing? she cried.

I was—

You're supposed to stay where I tell you. I thought I'd lost you.

But I was just—

Who is this? She glared at the other young boy who was dressed like a gypsy and standing with his back partly to her.

I think his name is Fausto, Oliver said. He's my friend.

Anna studied the boy closely. Dov' è tua famiglia? she demanded.

The boy glanced over his shoulder and did not answer.

Dov' è tua famiglia?

The boy looked at her.

Dove sono?

He pointed across the piazza and she looked where he pointed half-expecting to see a band of gypsies whose job it was to send their children out on freakish missions to steal and spread corruption on unsuspecting youth, possibly luring them away, never to be seen again unless it was for a great ransom. Those were the stories her mother had told her. That was how she'd been raised to think.

He's my friend, Oliver said again. We were just talking.

She looked at Oliver and she looked back at the gypsy boy, who was watching her with a mixture of contempt and misunderstanding. How do you know him? she asked.

What do you mean?

I mean did you know him before today?

No.

Anna looked again at the other boy. Do you speak English? she asked him.

Oliver answered, I don't think so.

She shot him a look. She wasn't quite through with him yet. You shouldn't have run off like that. I've told you before. You could easily get lost.

We were just talking, he said again.

Anna looked at the boy. Fausto, giusto?

The boy smiled and nodded his head.

Tore had come around the table too and he joined them and asked if everything was okay. She glanced up at him. I'm sorry, she said. I know you probably don't understand, but I worry that something could happen.

She guided Oliver back to the blanket and made him sit down and she told him that his friend could come too but when they turned to speak to him they found the boy had already vanished. I'm sorry, she said to Oliver. Then she went and sat down in her chair at the table.

Tore sat down beside her. She crossed her arms and glanced sideways at him.

Okay? he asked.

She didn't answer.

You are not used to a big city, he said.

She shook her head. She dabbed a finger at the corner of one of her eyes. Where we lived was nothing like here. Not at all. It was easier to keep an eye on things.

You lived in a small town?

I lived in a house, she said dryly.

Tore was silent a moment. He leaned over to get some things from a box he kept under the table and when he sat back upright he was holding a set of thicker brushes in his hand. Did you like it? he asked.

Like what?

Your house, he said. Was it nice?

She thought about it. It was just some stupid house.

Was it big like all American homes?

Can we talk about something else?

What would you like to talk about?

I don't know. Your uncle mentioned some festival.

Ah, yes, said Tore, La Festa Della Rificolona. What would you like to know?

Just tell me anything about it, she said.

-Monroe

Her team was losing 9–0. When he arrived she was sitting on the bench and he sat down in the bleachers near the entrance and watched the remainder of that match and the one that followed and when all of the matches had ended he stood and walked over and stood not far from where her mother was talking with some of the other parents. Carolyn spotted him and waved and motioned for him to come over but Monroe stayed put where he was.

A moment later the girls broke from their post-game huddle and Rebecca joined her mother, who pointed him out to her. She walked over.

Tough game, he said.

Not hardly.

But you played well.

Rebecca looked over her shoulder at her teammates, who were all moving toward the locker room. Monroe took the opportunity to glance over at her mother and he saw she was alone talking to a man holding a video camera connected to a tripod.

Who's that? he asked.

Rebecca looked. Just a guy she knows, she mumbled.

Monroe watched them. The man looked at his watch and then glanced at Monroe and said something to Carolyn and she looked his way too.

His name's Jack, Rebecca said.

Are they dating?

She didn't speak and Monroe looked over at her. She was staring down at the floor.

I'm sorry, he said. You don't have to answer that.

Forget it, she said. Besides, I'm the one who should be sorry.

For what?

She shrugged. I don't know. Them.

He touched her on the shoulder and then put his arm around her. You don't have to apologize for anything.

I didn't know he was coming or I would've said something.

Like what?

I don't know. Warned you, I guess.

Monroe grinned at her. Hey, he said. I'm a big boy.

Sometimes you aren't. At least that's what Mom says.

Monroe knew she meant it, but there was a little playfulness too in her voice and when she looked at him he saw the tiniest hint of a smile.

They laughed together then about it and he was thinking how good it felt to share a moment like that with her and was sad when it ended and she had turned back and looked toward the court and the smile had slid from her face. She looked at him. I probably need to go, she said. I'm sure the coach will have something to say.

All right, he replied. I'm glad I could make it.

Yeah, me too.

Will I see you at the Night Out?

I'm a little old for that, don't you think?

Maybe. It's just always been nice having you there. I'm bringing Grampa.

We'll see, she said. Some girls are getting together later.

Bring them along. There's plenty of photo and fingerprint kits.

I'm sure they'd love that, she said laughing.

Just think about it, he told her and she said that she would and as she was walking away he said that he would see her over the weekend and she waved at him and walked away. He watched her go and he thought there might be a chance he would see her later that night, but as the evening fell on the parking lot and the Night Out festivities began to wind down he realized he'd been mistaken.

He was standing beneath the blue sheriff's canopy not far from where his father sat in a folding lawn chair talking to another couple he'd gone to school with years ago. He watched them and wondered of the older man's capacity to remember something decades old but not the last time he had changed his shorts.

He gave the word for the two deputies to start packing up the camera and the identification kits and then he told his father he'd be right back and he walked down past the fire department and the K-9 unit to where a table and tent were erected for Mothers Against Drunk Driving. There an older man and woman were busy boxing up the materials they had brought.

Evening, Monroe said to them.

The two looked up. Why hello, Sheriff, the woman replied. How are you?

Good, Betsy. How was the evening?

That's where all the business went, the man grumbled. His kiddie card operation.

Oh, stop it, Liam, the woman said. It's not business. It's all for the good of the children. Isn't that right, Monroe?

That's true, but if you ask me, Monroe said, it's those national guardsmen who've been stealing the show.

They all three looked over at where the helicopter was sitting surrounded still by a crowd of children and adults.

By the number of gals in that bunch, Monroe went on, I'm beginning to think it's the uniforms not the chopper that's pulling them in.

How's that been working for you? Liam asked.

Monroe looked at him. About like it would for an ornery old judge, I expect.

If you two wisecracking men will excuse me, Betsy said, I need to speak to Martha Wyatt a moment. Can I trust you to take care of all this. She laid a hand on the back of her husband.

I think I can handle packing a box, he replied.

Betsy left and Monroe walked around the table to lend him a hand.

I've been reading some interesting things in the paper about you, Liam said. Have you done something to piss off the Eden Hill Sun?

Not that I know of, unless you consider canceling my subscription pissing off.

In this town, that qualifies.

Monroe folded up the legs of a tripod and carried it over and set it down in a little red wagon. I'm starting to think, he said, that it's just that way with politics. The other side finds your enemies and hands them a soapbox.

Son, it's been that way since before even Romulus killed Remus.

And those who would be blindsided have been taking it ever since.

The judge stopped what he was doing and looked at him. You all right?

Monroe shrugged and went back to his packing. He finished that box and set it in the wagon and asked, How did you know when it was time?

Time for what?

To resign.

I didn't resign, I retired. There's a difference. At least there is to me.

All right, then. How did you know when it was time to retire.

When Betsy told me it was time.

Monroe was quiet. He loaded the poster board next to the tripod and walked over to the table and picked up a box.

If I may, the judge said, I think what you mean to ask is how does one know whether to stay in public office or not.

All right.

The answer is I don't know.

That was very helpful.

Do you want the truth or only what'll make you feel better.

I'm kind of hoping they're the same.

Sorry to disappoint you, Monroe. But I was a judge for thirty years and I can count the number of times I thought about not wearing that robe on one hand and three of those came after Marcus was struck and killed. You know why that was? Because I knew that no matter how well or how poorly I did my job there was nobody better inclined or more dependable to do it than was I. Nobody. Think about it. If I had done something different twenty years ago when that good-for-nothing snake Bobby Shaw got his first DUI, just think how things might've turned out different. My son might still be alive. A thing like that weighs on you. It does. You think that with time it won't, but there's not a day goes by that it can't pull you right down under. But quit? No sir, not with the insight his death gave me. I'd have done that job forever if Betsy had let me.

Why did she want you to stop?

Why?

Yes.

The old man grew quiet. He stood up straight and looked out into the crowd as if searching for her that very minute. He looked over at Monroe. Sheriff, he said, there's only so much grief you can ask a woman to stand for.

-Anna

They didn't stay long at the market. When they heard from someone that the buses were up and running again Tore suggested that it might just be temporary so she decided to pack up and go and not risk another long walk with Oliver. She discovered though that only a few of the lines were running and so they could ride it only so far before having to walk the rest of the way.

A short distance from their piazza, Oliver complained of his legs hurting and they stopped to rest at the edge of a small grassy area. It was not far from their apartment building where there were benches to sit and where sometimes they'd come to eat baguettes and pecorino cheese or something from the gelateria and mingle and meet other young families from the neighborhood who had come for the treasured relief it delivered from their trying, tight quarters. Oliver had made many new friends there, of which none they saw now except for an older boy, probably twenty, who lived with his grandmother on the floor above them. He was playing fetch in the park with his dog. When Oliver saw them he asked could he go pet it.

I'd rather you not.

The boy overheard them and said, Non preoccuparsi, non morde.

He whistled at the dog and patted his hip and the dog trotted over and Oliver looked up at her and smiled.

Grazie, Anna said to the boy, ma dobbiamo andare.

Oliver tugged on her arm. Why can't I?

She looked at him. See, you do understand.

He said it wouldn't bite. Can I? Just for a minute, he pleaded.

For one minute.

Oliver ran over and knelt down and petted the dog and the boy spent a moment with him telling him things about it and pointing them out and then he stood and showed him how to throw the frisbee and she watched as Oliver took the disc in his hand and reared back with his arm and let go with all his might and the dog chased after it as it flew sideways into a grove of trees. The dog brought it back and Oliver threw it a few more times before she called to him and said it was time go.

Was that fun? she asked him.

Yes. Can we get a dog someday? he asked.

Someday, she replied.

He looked at her with surprise. Really.

She smiled. Really.

By then he had regained his leg strength and was skipping as they came into the piazza. He asked what they were having for dinner and she told him she wasn't sure, they would have to see what there was. What did you have in mind?

Hamburgers, he said.

Not hamburgers.

Why not?

For starters, I don't even know where you can get one.

We can ask someone. We can ask Giovanni.

They looked over and saw Giovanni closing his newspaper stand and Oliver ran to him and spoke to him and a moment later he turned and came running back to where she was waiting for him at the entrance to their building.

He doesn't understand, Oliver said.

That's fine, she said. It's been a long day. Let's just make pasta.

They walked to the door and she stopped to check their mailbox and found a folded white piece of paper in with the rest of the mail. She opened it and read it and then turned and looked at Giovanni who was watching them, smiling. She lifted the hand with the note and he nodded his head and pointed it toward the other side of the piazza where her uncle Alfredo sat watching them from a seat at an outdoor table at the coffee shop.

They walked together along the cypress-lined path leading to the Piazza dell' Isolotto enclosure in the Giardino di Boboli. Oliver was just ahead of them playing with a snow globe Alfredo had given him and when they passed through the tall iron gates that surrounded the moated island, she called to him to be careful.

Alfredo had brought a camera too amongst other gifts for them from her mother and he snapped a picture of Oliver and said, He is growing. Already he is taller, in just these past few months.

How is she? she asked.

Your mother? She is well. She misses you.

They sat down on a park bench while Oliver dipped his hands in the water. Anna opened the bag he had brought and peered inside, moving things around with her hand. There was candy, a cardboard puzzle. Some sort of ship captain's hat. She looked at him. She can't keep doing this.

What?

She took out the ship captain's hat. This.

Alfredo shrugged. She misses him.

I know she misses, but she can't keep doing this.

They're just things.

Things we don't need.

Alfredo snapped another picture. She wants to know when can she come see you, he said.

Anna looked at him queerly. Come see us?

Yes.

She wants to come see us? Here? In Florence?

That is what she asked.

Anna shook her head. Alfredo, you know she can't do that.

He lifted his shoulders. Maybe I could arrange something, he said There is talk of a possible evacuation on account of the hurricane. You've been following that?

She nodded.

Your mother thought if that happened she might come see you.

You can't be serious. She makes it sound like were on vacation here.

Anna suddenly turned and looked hard at him. You haven't told her where we are, have you?

No, of course not. She knows only that you are well and that on occasion I'm able to see you. She sees no reason she can't do so too.

Well, one big difference: no one really knows about you. We talked about this. She knew how hard it was going to be. She knew. And she agreed to it.

She will want to know when then.

I don't know when. It's not like I've done this before, Alfredo. There's not some magic timeline I'm following here. No. Anna shook her head. It's out of the question. You tell her she can forget it.

Che! Anna. She's your mother, she worries.

She worries? She knows nothing of this kind of worry, Alfredo. You know her. You know what she's like, how she can manipulate things. Don't let her. All this, she held up the bag, giving us these things, wanting to see us, it's not about us. It's all about her. It's always ever been about her, what she wants, what she needs.

She had raised her voice and looked around and saw a couple approaching. She waited till they walked past.

You're not her child, she said. You don't know her like I do.

People change, he said.

Yes, they do. I am trying to be an example of that right now and I can't do it without your help. There is not a day that goes by that I don't wake and wonder is this the end, is this the day they find us and all of it comes to an end. Is this the day I lose him for good. You want to talk about worry. I've got worries she can't comprehend, because she's never been willing to sacrifice anything for something she loved. Is she even aware of the danger of them finding us? Of what will happen then?

You know what will happen.

Yes, I do, she said. I just try not to think about it.

Book III

-Evan Meade

On Monday when Evan walked into his office he found
Azim waiting for him, seated across from his desk, his back
to the door. He set his briefcase on the floor next to the wall
and came around the desk and sat down in the swivel chair.
He looked at Azim. He waited for him to speak.

Feeling better? Azim finally asked.

Much, Evan replied.

Azim looked at his watch and looked up. He turned his
head and glanced behind him at the door.

Evan flipped the desk calendar to the right date and the
only note he saw scribbled there was a dental appointment
for Oliver. Nothing else. He looked over at Azim. Did I miss
something? he asked.

A shape darkened the doorway before Azim could
answer and the large round figure of Bryce Parker filled the
space.

Sorry, I'm late, Parker said. I got caught up with
something else. He shuffled in carrying a handful of papers
and parked himself in the other chair next to Azim. There
were tiny beads of sweat on his forehead and above his
upper lip. He seemed out of breath.

Azim looked at Evan. He said: Before you say anything,
I asked him to be here. Just to talk through the situation.

Good morning, Evan, the man from personnel chimed in. He wiped away the sweat with his hand and then wiped his hand along the seam of his pants. Azim brought me up to speed, he said, on the search for your missing son. It sounds like things are moving along nicely again and I just wanted to let you know that if there is anything we can do, anything at all, to assist in that endeavor, the bank is behind you one hundred and ten percent. That's not just me, speaking. That's from the top.

Parker paused and took a deep breath and then went on: For the moment, Azim thought it'd be good if the three of us sat down and just kind of went over how how things are going presently with you, your clients and such, you know, kind of get a read on where you are.

Where I am on what?

Parker shrugged. The beads of sweat had returned. He looked at Azim. Well, he said, on everything.

Evan studied him briefly. He looked at Azim. Is this about Philip Gardner?

It's not about any one client.

Azim's right, Parker added. This is more about you and your needs. To be sure, we appreciate how difficult this must be for you, the strain it must be on yourself and your current wife. Coming in here, having to focus on someone else's private affairs. No one would be surprised if it was starting to take a toll.

Evan looked at Azim. What is he even saying? Am I being terminated?

No, of course not.

Is this an official warning for some infraction?

No.

Am I being counseled, appraised, or offered any kind of promotion?

Azim no longer answered.

Then I don't understand, Evan said, why Human Resources is here?

He's here because I asked him to be here.

The three of them looked up at the door at the bank's founder, Jack Dillard. Parker started to stand but the old man made him stay where he was. I'll only be a minute, he said and he looked across the desk at Evan. You on board with this?

I don't know what this even is. They've been slow getting to it.

We just started, Parker added.

Well, hear them out, Dillard told Evan. I think you'll agree, it's what is right for both you and your clients, as well as this bank. At least until this thing is settled with your son. If nothing else, it'll give you a fresh chance to focus on that. Sound good?

Evan didn't answer, but the old man just nodded and said, Good, and after he left Parker looked at Azim and he looked at Evan. Here's what we're prepared to offer, he said. A three month leave of absence. Full pay and benefits. Check in once a week by phone. If after three months your son has still not been found, we'll review it again and see what can be worked out. Of course, once he is found you'll have plenty of time to reunite, get your legal affairs in order, et cetera. How's that sound to you?

Evan didn't answer.

Parker scooted to the edge of his seat and grunting heavily hefted himself from the chair. Here are the details in writing, he said. He handed Evan the sheet of paper. Look them over, sign them and then drop them off with Natalie. Your leave can begin as soon as you can arrange things with Azim. Today even, if that's possible.

Parker turned to go, then stopped and said, If you don't mind, Evan, let's not make a big deal of this, you know, with others. It might appear like preferential treatment. We wouldn't want that, would we?

After he left Evan sat staring down at his desk.

It's best for everybody, Azim said.

I need to think about it, Evan said.

Azim got to his feet. What's to think about? Look at it like a vacation.

Evan looked up at him. If you were to ask me, which no one did, I'd like to point out, I'd say it sounds like a severance package.

-Monroe

When Monroe walked into the library and asked for Grace it was the middle of the morning and the girl working the counter told him he could find her at the drugstore coffee shop. With all those other crazy red hats, she added.

He thanked him and went outside and since the weather was sunny and nice with a bit of a breeze he left the Blazer parked where it was behind the library and walked. When he came to the drugstore he went in and saw at once what the girl at the library had meant. Inside there were a dozen or so women of all ages, each wearing some fashion of a red hat and most clothed in some measure or other of purple attire. A little bell overhead had sounded when he entered and a table of them looked up at where he stood with his hand on the door and one of them muttered something and the table broke out in laughter.

He walked over. I see I've stumbled upon some kind of secret conspiracy, he said, looking around the room.

Grace sat grinning up at him. Sheriff, she said, then she looked at the others, I believe secret is the very definition of conspiracy. It's redundant to use both.

The other women laughed at this, to which Monroe replied, You'll have to excuse me. I wasn't aware this was a meeting of the Daniel Webster Fan Club. How is it this fanatic group has been right under my nose and I've not caught wind of it?

Because you're a man, someone said behind his back.

He turned to look and when he turned back around Grace had stood and was walking up to him and she took his arm in her own and said, Here, how about I rescue you from any further embarrassment, sheriff.

He walked with her outside into the bright sun. I assume you came there looking for me, Grace said. Or am I wrong?

I did indeed.

They headed up the street back towards the library with Grace's arm still wrapped in his and they did not speak for a long time.

Technically, Grace said, I'm not even supposed to be allowed in that group.

Not crazy enough? he asked.

Oh, I'm plenty crazy, just not old enough. You need to be over fifty to join. They only let me in because of my hair, I think.

I see.

They went on and after a while she said, I'm forty-nine, by the way. You didn't ask, but I'm forty-nine.

I didn't want to be rude.

But you thought it?

He smiled at her and shrugged.

See, she said, smiling back at him. Now you know.

They passed the Old Church with the canon ball from the civil war stuck in the brick over the entrance and she said, Honestly, I didn't expect to see you so soon.

He glanced at her. You said it was important.

I know, but I don't presume to think that what's important to me is the same as what's important to a sheriff.

Well, he said, I guess now you know too.

They both grinned and another moment of silence passed with them walking together and then she asked, Don't you want to know what it's about?

I do, he said, but for now, let's just enjoy the walk.

When they came to the library they walked up the steps and he held the door for her and she went in and he followed behind her and they sat down at the desk in her office. Grace pulled a sheet of paper from a drawer and handed it to him.

What's this?

It's a query, she said. Of that children's magazine you gave me.

Monroe leaned back in his chair to read. After he'd glanced over the list of names and addresses he put the paper down and looked at her. Who are they?

Well, Grace said. As you might imagine, the query I made of new subscribers in the last six months returned a much larger list than that one there. So I thought about something I'd heard, about most of her relatives coming from overseas, and so I altered the parameters to include only those subscriptions being mailed to an overseas address. You'll never guess what name popped up.

Which one?

The mother's. I mean not that mother, but the grandmother.

Monroe leaned forward and picked up the list and looked it over again.

There, Grace said and she bent over the desk and pointed. Right there. Elena Miller. She lives in Beaufort, South Carolina, correct? Anyway, I seem to remember that Beaufort is her home of record. But that's not all.

He looked over at her.

The billing address is Beaufort, but the magazine itself, it's mailed to an address in Belgium.

Did it return a name?

Is sure did. Someone named Alfredo Caruso. Does that mean anything to you?

Monroe shook his head. It's not one I've heard before.

Well, she said, maybe then that's a good place to start.

-Anna

They woke earlier than normal to meet Alfredo for breakfast before he was scheduled to leave and still leave plenty of time for the two of them to get to school. But by the time Oliver was ready though they were already running late.

I'm sorry. We can't stay long, Anna apologized as they walked up to the table outside the cafe and sat down.

It's no problem. Alfredo asked what they wanted to eat and he walked over and spoke at the counter and when he came back he reached into his travel bag and took out a magazine and handed it to Oliver.

What's this?

Something else your grandmother sends, he said. It comes in the mail. I almost forgot it.

Oliver looked at it and smiled. I used to get this, he exclaimed and he opened the magazine and started flipping through it.

Alfredo was happy too but when he looked at Anna he saw her frowning. It is just a magazine, he said. She has it sent to my house for him. He looked over at Oliver. Do you like it? he asked.

The boy nodded.

Can we save it for later, Anna told him. We need to eat and get to school. She looked pleadingly at Alfredo.

Yes, save it for later. Tell me about your school. You like it?

Oliver closed the magazine and shrugged. Not really.

Alfredo glanced at Anna and back at the boy. Why not?

I don't know. I just don't.

Alfredo looked again at Anna.

It's just taking some getting used to, she said.

It's a good school, no, Alfredo said. Giovanni said it was one of the city's best.

No, no, it's not the school, Anna said. The school is wonderful. She looked at Oliver. It's just, us. Being apart during the day.

A woman came over with a tray of coffee, a juice and pastries and set it down on their table. Anna passed it out and they started to eat.

And you? Alfredo asked her. You are happy with your work?

Yes, she nodded, but then said nothing more about it and casting her eyes downward wrapped both hands around the cup as if for its warmth and lifting it up took a sip. She set it back down. She looked at him. He was watching her. What? she asked.

He shook his head.

It's fine, she said and she offered a weak smile and when she saw how he was looking at her still without speaking she shook it off and said, Of course. I'm sorry, Alfredo. I'm being thoughtless. The school is wonderful, really. I can't thank you enough for everything you've done.

There are others, he said. Perhaps my friend could help place you in another. Perhaps the two of you together.

No, no, really, she said. I mean I'd like that and all but this one is fine. I'm sorry. I wasn't thinking. I like it, I do. My students are bright and seem eager to learn.

It was the only art teacher position in the city, he said. There were others, outside of Florence. In Arezzo, I think. Maybe Lucca. But I don't know if you would you want to consider those.

No, she said and glanced over at Oliver, who was eating, and she smiled. This is our home now, she said. She looked at Alfredo again and he seemed satisfied with that and so she changed the subject. When will we see you again?

Her uncle sat back in his seat and he raised his eyebrows elaborately. Well, I don't know. My work brings me here only on so often. I wish too I could come more but, you know. Business. It's why we chose Florence though, you remember. Because my work brought me here.

Yes. I remember.

Is there something you need? Something I can get you?

She shook her head. No, she said and she looked down at the table into the cup of coffee and the dark glistening surface there with little wafts of steam still rising and she said, It's just good to see someone else, you know. Someone who knows who we are.

When she looked up at him again her eyes had clouded over and she wiped at them and Alfredo stroked her shoulder. Neither spoke. They finished eating and collected their things and Alfredo said that he'd like to walk with them for a bit. If that's okay with you? he asked Oliver.

Oliver was sliding the children's magazine into his backpack and he looked up sharply and his face brightened. Maybe we'll see the boaters, he said.

Che? asked Alfredo.

Anna looked at him. La gente che pagaia su e giù per il fiume? she translated.

Ah, the canoisti. Sì, sì. I know of them.

But the only people on that water at that time of the morning were a couple of fishermen setting up their lines along the shore. Alfredo pointed them out from where they stood on the bridge to Oliver. Have you ever fished? he asked the boy.

No, he answered. I'd like to though.

I used to go all the time when I was your age.

Oliver looked up at him. You did?

Sure. Everyone in my neighborhood fished. My father, my brothers, even my mother.

Have you ever? Oliver asked his mother.

No sweetheart.

Why not?

I just didn't. No one ever took me.

Not your own daddy?

She shook her head.

Why not?

I don't know why, he just didn't.

Didn't he like fishing?

He liked to fish very much.

Just never did with you?

No. Apparently not.

What happened to him? How come I've never met him? Is he dead?

Anna looked at Alfredo before answering. No, sweetie, he's not dead. But he left me when I was little.

How little?

Very, she said. She led him by the hand across the bridge.

What was his name? Oliver asked.

Caesar, she said.

Caesar what?

Caesar Caruso.

Just like us? he said.

Yes, like us.

Alfredo looked at his watch. Hey, now. We'd better get going, he said, if I'm to see this sorry school of yours before I have to get on an airplane.

They went on with Oliver up ahead and Anna walking next to her uncle. She slid her arm into his. Okay? he asked her.

She nodded.

I am sorry for the bringing those things, he said.

Don't be, she said. It's just I don't see the point in giving him stuff that will remind him of a life he no longer can have. We're not those people anymore, Alfredo.

You can't ask him to just forget.

Not forget, she said. I don't want him to forget. Not ever. I just need him to be willing to move on.

-Evan Meade

After he'd signed the papers and turned them over to Parker's admin he left and was surprised when he arrived home to find Angela's car parked in the garage. He pulled in behind it and got out and went up to the house and opened the door and stepped inside. He saw her keys laying on the counter and he called to the house, Hello?

There was no answer. He listened for sound of her, then thought back to his leaving that morning and tried to remember the state of the house, the kind of shape in which he'd left it. A few dirty dishes still in the sink. Some laundry. An unmade bed. He went through the house, looking for her. In the living room he stopped and listened again and he could hear something, a noise, coming from behind him. It had an odd mechanical click to it. He followed the sound to the sliding glass door and looked out.

She was there, Angela, sitting on the patio at the end of one of the lounge chairs, her back was to him and beside her on the ground lay a kitchen paring knife. She wielded something in her other hand but he couldn't tell what that was. Between her legs sat the box he'd carried down from the attic and had not yet returned. He started to open the door then stopped and went down the hall very quietly and he looked into their bedroom and saw her suitcase lying open on the bed. It had been partially emptied it and he thought of her standing there in the room unpacking her clothes from the weekend, deliberating over the old box she'd seen in the hall, weighing the odds before deciding to look through it.

He went back to the living room and walked up to the sliding glass door and watched her through it. She reached into the box and pulled out a photograph and she held it up to look at it for a few seconds and then she lifted her other hand and touched something to the corner of the photo and there was smoke and a bright orange flame and he understood then that the thing she held in her other hand was the same butane lighter he'd used earlier to burn the garden brush pile.

The flame took hold and she gripped one small corner and then as the flame spread she dropped the picture on the floor atop a pile of dark downy ashes.

Evan pushed the door open and stepped onto the patio and closed it behind him. Angela didn't move. You came home early, he said.

She didn't answer.

He looked at the pile of ashes at her feet and took a step closer. I can see you've been busy.

Fuck you, she said and she lifted the letter he'd written to Anna and touched the lighter to it and the letter caught fire and when she could hold it no longer because of the flame she turned her face to look up at him but Evan had already left her. She dropped the letter and rose and came inside and she walked past him where he stood in the kitchen watching after and she went into the bedroom and slammed the door.

Evan followed her there. He opened the door and asked, what are you doing?

She was stuffing clothes into her suitcase. What do you think I'm doing? she said. I'm leaving.

You just got home.

She took out a pair of shoes to make some more room in her bag. Her breathing was heavy as she labored to make it all fit.

Evan watched her. It was just an old box, he said.

Then you won't mind my having burned it. She went over to her dresser and pulled open a drawer and gathered more things. Socks. Rolled up balls of panties. That's not even all of it, is it? she asked.

All of what?

What you've kept of her.

That was everything.

I don't mean just a letter and some stupid pictures.

He didn't say anything. He just watched her stomping back and forth from the dresser to the bed, shuttling handfuls of belongings, shoving them into the pockets, stuffing the corners, anywhere she could find to fit more in. He did not ask her to stop, nor did he go and just leave her to it. He watched it all from the doorway, her every move, and when she had finished and crossed in front of him dragging the suitcase behind her he reached out and took hold of her arm.

Let go, she said.

You're being ridiculous.

She glared at him. Am I? You don't even know how much I wish right now that she'd said yes. She's smarter than I gave her credit.

Evan shoved her and she fell hard on her belly against the bed. She rolled over and glared at him and started to get up and he pushed her again and she lay half on half off the bed. Get away from me, she growled, her voice not sounding like her own.

He loomed over her. He looked her in the face and he looked down at her legs where they disappeared beneath the short hem of her denim skirt. her white panties showing below.

You can forget that, she said and she lifted both legs and kicked at him.

He grabbed one of her feet and bent it and she screamed and he worked his hand around her leg to get a better hold of it and he twisted it, rolling her on to her belly.

Goddammit, Evan, I swear. Her face was shoved into the mattress, her sound compressed, muffled.

He felt the urge to climb on top of her but he let go and she wiggled around and scrambled to her feet. She was breathing hard and glaring at him. You are such a fucking asshole, she said.

She stomped past him and grabbed the handle of the suitcase and dragged it behind her into the hall. A moment later a door somewhere slammed shut.

Evan went to the window and he watched her leave and afterwards he went and sat at the kitchen table and he took out his wallet and called the toll free numbers listed on the backs of their credit cards. To whoever answered he reported them stolen and asked that they deny any further activity. Then he called the bank and requested a wire transfer of all of their funds to an individual account he'd opened without her knowledge just a few short weeks earlier.

-Monroe

It was close to dinnertime when Monroe pulled into the little country store and so after he filled the Blazer with gas he went inside and when he came out again he was carrying a couple of bottles of soda and four hotdogs wrapped in tinfoil. He drove just a short bit further down the road and pulled into the apartment complex.

The lady inside at the desk smiled at him and saw what he had in his hands and said, Why, Sheriff, what a pleasant surprise. Now won't he be delighted.

Monroe walked down the hallway and up the stairs to the second floor and when he came to door number 212 he stopped and knocked on it.

His father opened the door. He was wearing his pajamas and when he saw who it was he stuck out his head and looked both ways down the hall. What are you doing here? he asked Monroe. Something wrong?

Nothing's wrong, Monroe said. I just thought I'd stop by. See how you were.

What's that there?

Hotdogs.

One for me?

You bet.

They went inside and his father went back and got a robe from his bedroom and came back out and sat down at the little table in the kitchen. Monroe was looking for plates.

In the cupboard there. There might be some chips in there too if you're interested.

I'm fine, unless you want them.

No. This'll be enough. I just ate dinner a while ago.

They ate their hotdogs and drank their sodas and shortly after they'd finished they were sitting there talking about the dogs when they heard a siren outside. They both turned their heads to listen.

Fire, his father said.

They waited for the engine to pass, the siren's tone changing only briefly as the driver paused for safety's sake before sweeping through the intersection out in front of the apartments.

The old man looked at Monroe. You feel like watching some television? They got just about every station you'd ever want to watch at this place. Somewhere they probably even got porn.

I don't think so, Dad.

No. You should see how some of these women behave. Couldn't hold a stick to your mother though, especially not in that department.

All right, Monroe said and stood up. What do you feel like watching?

The news, what else.

Monroe walked over and picked up the remote and came back and sat down on the couch next to where his father had settled in the recliner.

Any particular news?

I don't care. Whichever one you watch.

I don't watch any.

You don't?

Nope. Don't even own a T.V.

You're mother hated the television too. Called it an idiot box. What do you do then to pass time?

I don't really know, Monroe said. I guess I've not got that much time that needs passing.

Wish I had your problem. Here, there's nothing but time.

Come on now. They do some fun things around here.

Sure. If you're into karaoke. The truth is, I've about had all I can stand of it.

Monroe looked at him. Let's not talk about that right now. Tell me a number, he said and pointed the remote at the T.V.

-Anna

The school day was almost over when the secretary at her school came to get her from class for a phone call. It was Oliver's school. He had an upset stomach and she needed to come get him.

She asked were they sure it was not just something he ate, perhaps one of the treats one of the other parents was always bringing in, but the school assured her he'd eaten nothing since arriving that morning. He'd be packed up and waiting in the secretary's office for when she got there.

Anna made the necessary arrangements with her own classes and and gathered her purse and things and went outside. The sky was gray and windy, a dark rotund body of clouds lurking to the east desperate for the city's broad plain and level ground. To the west the sun's light was in full retreat, the white-gold streaks of color pouring out under the battered clouds. She stood with her back to the school, enjoying briefly, solely, the violet colored rapture until from across the street an old woman flung open the sash and leaned from her window to retrieve the laundry hanging there to dry, her eyes angry and darting upward ablaze with hostility toward the sky. The ground shuddered beneath the far thunder.

Someone walked up behind her and she turned and saw the principal, Nicola Bonelli, standing there. He was smiling. More rain, he said.

It seems so, Anna said.

He looked at her purse, the satchel of papers she was carrying. Leaving?

My son is sick, she said. His school called.

I hope it's not severe.

It sounds like just a stomach bug.

He looked again at the things she was carrying. Can I help you with those? he asked.

No, she said, looking out over the steps leading down to the courtyard and the street below. I can manage.

He is doing better with school, yes?

Yes, she nodded and looked at him. He seems to be.

It takes time, learning to adjust to new things. Children, especially, can be easily frightened by things they don't understand.

The principal lit a cigarette. He smoked and studied the approaching storm. Tell me about your last teaching assignment.

She looked at her watch. I really need to be going.

You taught in America, correct?

Yes, she answered.

And your son's father. What does he do?

He doesn't live with us, she said.

He did not come with you?

No he did not.

You are separated or divorced?

Divorced.

Across the way the woman finished taking her clothes off the line. She pulled her head back in the window and drew her shutters closed. It began to rain.

I really must go, Anna told him but the principal did not pay her any attention. He was watching a scrawny black kitten where it had appeared at the corner of the school building. The cat darted up the steps and stopped under the overhang and sat down and lifted its paw to lick. The principal clicked his tongue and the animal stopped abruptly, its paw poised in the air, and then without even a glance their way, it turned and darted back down the steps into that wet weather.

Nicola looked at her and raised his eyebrows. Would you like to get some coffee? he asked.

She hesitated as if not sure she understood his question correctly. I'm sorry, she said, but my son. He's sick. I need to go get him.

Of course. I understand completely. Perhaps I can give you a ride then.

That's really not necessary, she said.

I insist.

Anna looked from beneath the roof and at the sky. I'm sorry. I have to go, she said and pulled the hood of her rain jacket over her head and hurried down the steps.

That night, she was sitting alone at the table working under the light when Oliver came shuffling down the hall in his footed pajamas. Feeling better? she asked.

Some, he said.

Are you hungry?

He looked at what she was working on. He picked up a sheet of colored tissue. What are you doing?

It's just something I thought we could do together.

What is it?

It's a lantern.

What's a lantern?

You know, you put a candle in it so it lights up the dark.

You make that out of paper?

These kind you do.

What kind?

For that festival coming up, she said. Giovanni and Tore have been talking about it. You know those posters we've seen around town. It's called La Festa Della Rificolona.

What's that mean?

The Festival of the Lanterns. Doesn't that sound fun? We'll make ours out of papier-mâchè using a balloon and other art stuff and when we're finished we'll be able to put a candle in it. That night at the festival then all the kids carry their lanterns on a long stick and sing songs.

Songs about what?

She thought about it. Poor people, she said.

That doesn't sound very fun, or nice. He laid the tissue paper down on the table and walked over to the TV and asked could he watch it.

Don't you want to eat?

I'm not really that hungry.

She stood and walked over and felt his forehead. You should eat something.

Just for a while, he said.

What do you want to watch? she relented.

Cartoons.

I don't think we'll find them at this time of the day.

She turned on the TV and using the remote skipped through the channels until she came to one with a clear image.

That's the news, Oliver said.

I know.

The picture it showed was of a beach somewhere, there was heavy wind, rain, various images of destruction. She turned it up and listened to the anchor describe the scene.

The eye came ashore at around four o'clock this morning, he was saying, moving at about sixteen miles per hour, passing roughly ten miles north of this point where I'm standing now near the barrier resort islands. Then it turned northward and headed up the coast toward North Carolina. According to the National Weather Service winds here at Beaufort reached 120 miles per hour.

Mom?

Just a minute.

Flash flood warnings have been posted, all up and down the coast, from Florida to Virginia. Officials had already issued a mandatory evacuation order for the coast of South Carolina and northern Georgia but many residents chose not to heed the order and now a good number of those who remained are fleeing the devastation.

Where is that? Oliver asked.

It's home, she said.

Who's home?

For a while it used to be mine.

-Evan Meade

Evan lay on the couch with his feet propped up watching the twenty-four hour news channel. He had the sound muted but the images said enough. Homes blown over. Trees and power lines down. Standing water everywhere. Entire neighborhoods wiped out. The marina they showed looked like a war zone and the streets held the detritus of the hurricane's destruction. People were trickling out from their hiding places, survivors emerging from homes with tears filling their eyes and holding tightly to one another, cradling their children for love or support or both.

The phone rang. He did not get up to answer it.

Angela's voice came over the answering machine. Thank you, you fucking ass, she said and hung up.

He turned up the volume. They were talking about the damage done to a nearby zoo and of the intensive effort underway to corral the zoo's animals. They talked of the various sea creatures that were lining the beaches, injured or dead. They talked of the relief effort underway and of the electrical work crews coming from as far as Alabama and Tennessee, responding to the emergency call to restore power. They talked of how food and shelter was the primary worry. They talked of the dead and of the dying and of how none of those names had yet been released, pending notification of next of kin.

-Monroe

Monroe walked in to the annex and said good morning and asked Jeannie if she could see about getting Elena Miller on the telephone.

You heard?

I heard.

I can try, but the phones are probably down.

Do me a favor and just try. Monroe went into his office and sat down at his desk. He dialed the number for the FBI office in Charlotte and left a message with Agent Forster.

A moment later, Jeannie appeared at the door. I hate to say it.

Nothing?

Nope.

I figured as much. Did you try the sheriff?

I'll do that next.

Monroe was watching her but it was as if he was looking right through her and not at her at all. She'd seen that look before and stood waiting.

After a few seconds he looked her in the eye. Let me ask you something, he said. Say you knew someone you cared about was in danger. How far would you go to try and find out if they were okay?

Depends, Jeannie said, pretty far if I really needed to know, or if they were truly that important to me.

Say it was someone you'd planned on never seeing or speaking to again or for a very long time.

Can we stop pretending you're not talking about Anna Miller?

Monroe didn't answer. He sat there a very long time.

I know what you're thinking, Jeannie said finally. You want me to put in a request for one of the county's cars?

Not particularly.

I can try the airlines.

All right. But nothing too expensive.

What's too expensive?

You'll know when they tell you.

How soon you wanting to leave?

Soon as possible.

Today?

Probably not today. Tomorrow's fine.

Jeannie walked back to her desk.

He thought of something else. And when you get a chance, he said, bring me Evan Meade's work number.

That name doesn't ring any bells? Monroe asked him. They were sitting at the dining room table. It looked to be the only place in the house to sit that wasn't covered with the wash.

Meade shook his head.

You never heard her mention it?

Not that I can remember.

Maybe from before you got married, or at the wedding? Somebody there as a guest?

It was just us.

You got married at the courthouse?

Meade didn't answer right away. It was better that way, he said.

Better why?

A wedding would have taken time to put together.

Sorry. I don't understand. Why the hurry? Lots of women I know planned their weddings for several months. I knew one who took three years.

Meade looked at him and he looked away and he looked over again at the sheriff. She was pregnant.

And she was afraid she'd be showing.

Meade nodded. Only by a few weeks, I think.

That's still a bit much to keep covered up. There's people who'd do the math if they really wanted to know.

Well, she wasn't too keen on the alternative.

The alternative?

Meade looked at him. The alternative to having a baby, he said.

Were you?

I don't see how that's relevant. Meade stood up. Sorry I couldn't be of more help. Is there anything else we need to talk about?

Monroe got to his feet. He pushed his chair up. He looked around at the messy house. I was surprised to find you at home today, he said. This is not some new bank holiday, is it?

Just taking some time to help around the house, Meade said.

Monroe looked at him. Your wife must really appreciate that.

I guess you'd have to ask her.

-Anna

When she woke it was a full hour ahead of the alarm. She lay curled on her side looking at the window and into the pitch black dark beyond. There were no sounds. No bakers. No deliverymen. No nothing.

She drew her legs to the edge of the bed and sat up and looked over where the boy's hair poked out of the covers, then she got up and went to the kitchen. She set a pot of coffee to brew on the stove and then thought of the time and turned the stove off and just stood there then, waiting for something else to come to mind. Some task that needed doing. When nothing did she went and turned on the TV.

In the last day there'd been little news out of South Carolina. What with the hurricane occurring in the undistinguishable North American Mid-Atlantic the event commanded only two days of coverage on Italian television. Even the papers, which lagged a day behind, were writing of the storm in the notably past tense. Something unfortunate that had come and then gone.

What she did know was that the storm had spent itself over South Carolina then curved north brushing the North Carolinian barrier islands and was now headed out to sea. The news had been good for telling her that. And it was good for showing pictures of the damage. Downed power lines, fallen trees. Flooded roadways and houses. Images of emergency personnel working to restore the area to normalcy. What it hadn't given her was what she most needed to see. A list of those dead or injured. The names of the missing. Those who had lost their homes and possessions. Of what had become of her mother.

When it came time to wake Oliver for school, she slipped on a pair of sweatpants and a jacket and slipped out of the apartment and went downstairs to the piazza and called her school from one of the public phones. She left a message saying that Oliver was still not feeling well and she needed to miss that day. Then she hurried back up the stairs.

They spent the day inside, flipping between the news and Oliver's cartoons. She did not explain to him what had happened and he didn't ask. As the day wore on and what little news that filtered in revealed less and less information she found other things to occupy them. Reading. Coloring books. The lantern project.

Halfway through the design of it Oliver left her alone to it and since it was early she left his work in disarray on the table, thinking he might come back to it. He didn't and by lunch time, the house looking a total mess and the evening a long way off, she wished they'd went ahead and just gone to school.

-Monroe

Monroe watched the girl across from him at the counter of the rental car place stand there clicking through and reading the computer monitor. He set his bag down on the floor. How soon before you'll have one for me? he asked.

Tomorrow most likely.

But the reservation is for today, not tomorrow.

She looked at him, then back at the computer. I know, sir, I'm sorry. There's not a car available.

What are those out there? He glanced sideways out the window at the few vehicles sitting on the lot.

Those are already leased.

Thank you. So was mine.

The girl looked over at the door to the manager's office where an older black woman sat looking at them from behind a desk. The woman looked very tired and unhappy. She stood and came out and without speaking stepped in front of the computer and started typing. She looked at Monroe. What's the confirmation number?

The girl handed her a slip of paper.

It's not here, the woman said after she entered it.

I know it's not there, said the girl.

The woman ignored her and typed something more. It's because this reservation was taken at a different office. She looked across at Monroe. Your car is in Beaufort, she said. This is Savannah.

I know where I am, Monroe said.

That's why we don't have a car for you.

Monroe took out his phone and started to call Jeannie back at the office.

There is one other option, the woman said, gazing at the computer monitor.

The passenger van seated twelve, like one of those used by church groups, and about the only good thing he could say about it was that thankfully he wasn't the one driving it. The traffic between the two coastal towns was heavy. There were lines of cars both coming and going, but mostly they were headed in his same direction.

The damage along the route was scattered and unpredictable. The most visible signs of loss were broken and uprooted trees, the occasional flooded creek. Most of the structures he saw in the area were still standing. As he got closer to Beaufort the destruction was greater, though even then there seemed no logic to the hurricane's mayhem, no pattern of destruction that helped him understand why the storm took pity on one area and ruined the next beyond recognition.

In Beaufort he picked up his rental and a map of the area and he headed down Gloucester Street to where it intersected Bay and then followed the signs for the Waterfront Park where he saw crews out working with chainsaws and men in tan jumpsuits from a prison work group picking up fallen debris and loading it into a dump truck. A fat prison guard stood watching over them, the butt of his shotgun poised on his hip. Another guard squatted nearby. Over the street hung a large blue and white banner announcing the Beaufort Stewbilee. Beyond was a fleet of shrimp boats docked in the still dark water of the harbor.

Monroe slowed and studied the map. He checked it against the road signs, then went on. Six blocks from the park he found the street he was looking for and turned down it. Elena Miller's house was at the end of a cul-de-sac and appeared, other than one fallen tree, to have gone unscathed. Some missing shingles. A boarded up window. Other than that, not much looked out of place. Even the tree had already been sawed into smaller sections and the brush piled near the curb.

He parked the car in front of her mailbox and stepped out into the bright sunlight. It was almost three p.m. He looked up at the cloudless blue sky then over at the house. He heard in the distance more chainsaws, a wind chime blowing somewhere, the rattle of palmetto leaves, and he walked past the brush pile and the fallen tree and came up the steps to the porch.

The house was open. He cupped his hands and looked in through the screen door and past the small foyer down the long hallway that passed down the center of the house. It emptied onto the kitchen. To the right was the dining room and just beyond that were stairs leading up to a second floor landing. He knocked. Hello, he said.

A sound came from his left and he turned and followed the porch around the corner of the house and leaned over the railing. He caught himself looking straight down on top of someone's gray head. The woman was bent down, talking to something under the porch. Copper, come here, she was saying, her voice thick with a foreign accent. Copper! She slapped her hand against the lattice work.

Excuse me, Monroe called down to her.

The woman startled and turned her head skyward and she grimaced from the bright sunlight and lifted her hand to shield her eyes and she said, Who's there?

I'm sorry, he said. Don't be alarmed. I'm Monroe Rossi. From North Carolina.

The woman stood up straight. She looked at him closer. What do you want?

Is everything all right? he asked.

It's the dog. She pointed under the porch. He's under there and I need to get a ladder.

To get him out.

No, to fix the back deck.

And the ladder is under the porch?

Precisely.

The woman dropped to both knees and turned her attention to the area beneath the porch. She called to the dog again. Come here Copper!

Monroe walked back the length of the porch and came down the steps and he went over and crouched down beside her. There was a dog lying curled up against the exposed cinder block foundation just a few feet away. The ladder lay behind the dog, which looked scared. Hey, there, he said to the animal. He looked at the woman. Won't he move if you just reach in and drag it out?

Maybe. You want to try it?

That is your dog, right?

Technically? No. He's just a stray. But I've seen him around a bit. She looked at the dog. He seems harmless enough, don't you think?

He won't bite?

No, he won't bite.

Monroe peered under the porch at the dog. He looks like he would.

He shouldn't. I feed him often enough.

But he looks like he might.

Oh, for crying out loud.

The woman made to move in front of him and Monroe raised his hand. No, I'll get it, he said.

He reached in slowly for the ladder with one hand. Good boy, he kept saying over and over to the dog. Good boy. Just going to get this thing out of your way, he said as he slowly wrapped his fingers around the wooden ladder. He started to pull it toward him when the animal lunged.

The bite had barely broken the skin and the dog retreated instantly, but so sudden and ferocious was his attack that Monroe jerked away abruptly and banged his head into one of the overhead beams. Dammit! he cursed and looked over his shoulder at the woman. I thought you said he wouldn't bite.

What'd you do to him?

I didn't do anything.

You must've scared him somehow. The woman leaned under the porch and cooed. What's the matter, little fella? This mean old man scare you?

Monroe touched top of his head and felt wetness and pulled his hand away and found it smeared with blood. The woman saw it too and rose to her feet and checked his head and then his hands. It's not that bad.

It's bleeding.

It's not like you need stitches or anything. I'll get a bandage and the hydrogen peroxide.

It's fine, Monroe told her.

Just come with me, she told him and she led him to the front door. She made him wait in one of the chairs while she went in to get a first aid kit. She doctored his head, then his hand and when she had finished she looked at her handy work and said, Good as new.

Monroe flexed the fingers of his injured hand. I guess it'll have to do.

The woman rolled her eyes. That sounds like the beginnings of a law suit.

I thought the dog wasn't yours?

He isn't, but the ladder is.

Don't worry, he told her. If I'd wanted you arrested I would have done it already.

The woman looked at him warily.

It's Monroe, he said. Monroe Rossi. I'm the sheriff from Eden Hill.

She nodded and looking confused sat down in the other chair.

Monroe took a good look at her, saw how the skin around her cheeks and eyes was darker, shadowed and sun-dried tough, but the color of her eyes matched her daughter's precisely. Pools of burnt almond, reminders of autumn. The high cheek bones, the narrow chin. It was everything he'd expected of Elena Miller.

You're wasting your time, she said to him. I don't know where she is.

She picked up the things she had used to bandage him and started putting them into the first aid kit. And shame on you, she said as she got to her feet, for trying to trick me.

Monroe stood too. I wasn't trying to trick you, he said.

What do you call that then?

Trying to help.

So you came all the way down here from North Carolina just to lend an old woman a hand.

No ma'am.

What are you doing here then?

Honestly, he said, I'm not really sure.

Looks to me like you're following one disaster up with another. I've already told you. I've told them all, everyone. I don't know where she is.

You've not heard from her?

No.

Not a word just to hear you're okay?

I can take care of myself. She knows that.

Does she know the boy's father has hired someone to track them down? A private investigator.

Isn't that your job?

He must have thought I needed some help.

Sounds like you've got it then. Good-bye, Sheriff. She turned and opened the door and went inside and let the screen door slam behind her.

Monroe turned and looked out at the street. He heard the dog moving around under the porch and was about to head down the steps to fetch the ladder for her when the door swung back open. Elena stepped back onto the porch. There is one thing I'm wondering though, now that you've said it. Why did you tell me about him hiring that investigator.

He shrugged. I thought you should know.

So I could warn her?

No ma'am.

Then why?

So you could use it to sell her on coming back on her own.

Coming back? Elena stood there holding the door opened with one hand looking at him. Sheriff, she said, my daughter and her son are exactly where they need to be, wherever that is. People need to just let them be.

I can't do that.

You mean you won't.

Won't? Can't? It's the same thing.

Not for her.

It should be.

She let the door swing shut and turned to face him. You've never had something done to you that was wrong?

Sure I have. Everybody has.

Did you do something about it?

I see where you're going with this but there are rules that need to be followed.

Those two belong together.

That's for a judge to decide.

You're just like the rest of them, she said. Don't come down here talking to me about judges. Judges don't know everything.

No ma'am they don't.

You don't even know her. You only know what you've been told.

If I could talk to her I'd likely form my own opinion.

And that would help?

I don't know. I can tell you that kidnapping isn't exactly helping her cause.

What cause? There's no cause, Sheriff. You're looking at this all wrong.

How am I looking at it?

Wrong, she said.

In what way?

You're thinking that maybe there's some piece missing to all this that'll explain it. I've already told you everything you need to know. All she wants is her little boy. That's all she ever wanted. You want to talk about rules and judges and such. You need to take a long look at where those things got her. You know what advice her attorney gave her before they ever went to court?

No ma'am I don't.

Clean hands. That's what she said. She said it was important they didn't cast aspersions against Evan. She told her judges can see right through that tactic and might think you're just out to get him.

I can appreciate how that might backfire.

Can you?

He didn't answer.

It was stupid advice. Clean hands don't make any difference. The legal system is full of parasites, sheriff. Judges, lawyers, they thrive on dirt and grime. They eat it, swear by it. They lather in mud and make love to themselves while sprawled on heaping mounds of it. Dirty hands win lawyers cases. Everyone knows that, even you.

There are some that are different.

Those that are don't stay lawyers for long.

Some do, he said.

There's another thing you probably don't know. When the judge told her he was taking away her son he put it like this: In my legal opinion—that's how he began, his Honor— in my legal opinion, what's in the child's best interest. As if law and raising a child are somehow connected. Do you know what that felt like to her, his mother? After days of testimony, months of waiting, of putting up with all the lies and so much suffering, this was what she got: In my legal opinion, what's in the child's best interest. As if she didn't know better. She went to that court with the cleanest of hands and after all was said and done, all she had to show for it then was liberal visitation. You know who else gets visitation, Sheriff? Prisoners.

What of the appeals court?

What of it. It got her nothing. A few extra days through the year, big fat deal.

Well, I don't know what to say, said Monroe. Thank you for sharing that.

You're welcome. I feel better. But that's not what you came here to talk about is it?

No ma'am, it isn't.

You know I can't help you.

I know.

Then why come all this way?

He thought about it and said, I guess I just needed to see for myself.

-Anna

The train car shuddered and bucked along the tracks. Outside it was getting dark and she sat stroking Oliver's head where it lay in her lap as he slept. Across the aisle a young boy sat next to a little girl reading a book to her. The girl wore a blanket over her legs. When the porter came by to check their tickets and ask did they need anything the boy shook his head. He closed the book and put it away and turned off the light above the seat, then he pulled the blanket around her shoulders and sat with her snuggled up against him, his arm around her, until he too fell asleep.

Anna looked out the window at the countryside. Watching the last little bits of daylight trickle and fade. Every where long low stretches of orchards and vineyards crept beneath the dark shadow of night and the hills shone the color of rose hips, where the barns and the houses and factories built there were all lavender-tinted, the latter sprouting amongst the growing fields like a grand mirage in that twilight hour. There were lights glowing in all of the houses, bearing proof of their occupancy, those who were likely settling down after meals of fried gnocchi, prosciutto and bottles of wine to retire to their beds until morning, when they would greet once again the great Apennine

Mountains that rose and spilled and toppled all around them with what appeared reckless abandon.

It was well after nine when the train pulled into the station at San Salvatore. She woke Oliver. He looked at her and looked around at the boy and his sister and then he looked at the other passengers and stood up as if to deboard with them but then asked in a thick, scratchy voice to be carried.

Outside it was spitting rain and she set him down on the curb with their bags and the boy shivered against her leg while she hailed a taxi. The driver loaded the bags and she helped Oliver into the back seat where he fell back asleep and only after she gave the directions to the driver did she let herself relax.

She closed her eyes. She might have gone to sleep but it was not far to her grandmother's house and so if she had slept it wasn't for long. The driver woke her and she opened her eyes and sat up and looked though the rain streaked window at the house in the tiny neighborhood where it sat on the outskirts of town. There were no lights on and in the dark it looked the same as when she had lived there as a child, though it looked much smaller now than what her memory recalled. The street, Via Petra, looked smaller, too, narrower than what she'd remembered.

Stai bene? the driver asked her.

She looked at him.

He was watching her in the mirror.

She got out and hurried around the cab and opened the door on Oliver's side and she leaned in and collected him from where he laid slumped across the back seat. The driver retrieved her luggage from the trunk and he set the bags on the wet sidewalk and got back out of the drizzle and into his cab. He rolled down the window and she paid him and then with her son in her arms she turned and faced the dark house. She left the luggage where it was and walked up to the wrought iron gate. She shifted Oliver in her arms and wiggled a hand loose and found the gate's latch and lifted. The latch moved a little, but the gate did not open. She wiggled it harder, then brought Oliver to her ear and whispered his name.

Honey, she said when he did not answer and she shook him just slightly until he stirred. I need you to wake just a minute, she said. I need your help.

Somewhere down the street a dog started to bark.

I'm going to have to lift you over this fence. I need you to stand up.

He nodded.

She lifted him to a level she thought would adequately clear the fence edge and she said to him, Are you ready?

Oliver didn't answer. He'd fallen back asleep. She shook him gently again. Oliver? Are you awake?

Okay, he said.

Through the dark a voice yelled after the dog and the dog stopped barking.

She lifted him again and pressed up against the fence and started to lower him down. His feet dangled until they touched soil. There, she said to him. Now stand back.

It was only raining a little but their clothes were getting soaked and so she tried to be quick about it as she set the bags over the fence and started to reach one leg over. She was straddling the fence when a car passed by. She froze. The headlights approached and then the car passed and with little haste she lifted her other leg over and snatched Oliver up in her arms and hurried up to the door.

She knocked. Several minutes passed before anyone came to the door. The porch light came on, blinding them, and then her grandmother opened the door. She was dressed in her robe and looked roused from bed and for a brief instant her eyes settled on the two standing at her door without assimilation.

Ciao, Nonna, Anna said.

The eyes of the old woman grew wide with recognition. She waved them into the house. Entri, entri.

Anna squeezed by her and went and laid Oliver down on the sofa and she covered him with a blanket and went back to where her grandmother was standing watching them. Scusami, Nonna, she said. E ' così tardi. She hugged her.

Non importa, said the woman. She looked over at Oliver. Vuoi metterlo al letto?

Anna said that his bed could wait and she went to the door and opened it and went outside and came back in carrying the bags and she set them down on the floor. She took off her coat and went into the kitchen and hung it on a hook near the back door among the out of fashion garden slickers, heavy coats and various forms of bonnets. Her grandmother came in behind her.

Siediti, siediti, she said and motioned for her to sit.

Anna sat.

Vuoi un caffè?

While they waited for the coffee to brew they sat at the table and talked, the old woman patting her hand and smiling. Her eyes looked much more solitary and enameled than what Anna had remembered.

Com'è andato il vaggio? the woman asked.

È stato molto difficile, Anna said.

The old woman nodded. Specialmente con un piccolo.

She stood then and came slowly around the table, touching each chair as she passed for balance. She opened the cabinet to the right of the sink and took out a porcelain plate and she unscrewed the cap from a jar on the counter and reached in and took out a handful of wafer cookies and laid them on the plate. She carried it to the table and set it down in front of Anna. Ti ricordi di queste? she asked.

Anna smiled up at her and nodded. Si, si, Nonna. Mi ricordo.

She took one and broke off a piece and put it in her mouth and the taste did indeed remind her of childhood. She stood and poured them both a coffee and sat back down.

Her grandmother asked about her mother. Non ho parlato con da po', she said.

Hai provato a telefonare?

No, no, Nonna said. She frowned and rubbed the tips of her wrinkled old fingers together. Il telefono è troppo caro.

Anna watched her. She reached out and touched her hand. Her grandmother looked at her and they both smiled. Forse mentre io sono qui, Anna said.

Her grandmother nodded. She started to get up to get the phone, but Anna stopped her. Domani, Nonna, she said. Domani.

Bene, bene, the old woman replied and she settled back down in her chair.

They finished their coffee and afterwards Anna went and gathered Oliver in her arms to carry him up to bed. She had wanted to ask what opinion her grandmother had of what she'd done with him, of taking and keeping him from his father, but she did not. It wasn't until later, after she was putting herself to bed, when her grandmother came shuffling in to the tiny bedroom and asked how was her husband, that Anna realized no one had even told her.

-Monroe

Monroe was sitting in a diner at a table with the sheriff of Beaufort County and his adult son eating breakfast when a bus pulled up to the station across the street. He watched through the window where the people were stepping down out of the door and onto the sidewalk. He was looking at each of their faces.

You think she'll show up here? the sheriff asked.

I doubt it. Monroe turned and looked forward. Who really knows though, he said. There are some people who can let go of the past completely and there are those who cannot.

The question is which one is she.

Your guess is as good as mine.

The waitress came over and offered to refill the coffee. They all three declined and she left the check tableside. Monroe picked it up and slid it into his shirt pocket. The sheriff thanked him and said, I don't suppose the grandmother was much help?

She didn't seem all that much interested in talking about it.

She get any damage?

A few lost shingles, a broken window. Mentioned something about her back deck.

I'll send someone over to check it out. Maybe the spirit of help and cooperation will loosen her up some.

Maybe. You know her?

The sheriff shook his head.

What about the girl?

What about her?

They moved here when she was still a teenager. I thought maybe one of you remembered something about her from back then. Monroe looked over at the sheriff's son. She's probably about your age, he said.

I knew of her, the boy said simply.

The two men sat looking at the younger man.

I didn't know her that well, he said.

The two of you friends? his father asked.

I wouldn't call it that.

What would you call it?

I'd say I knew of her.

What about others she hung around? Monroe asked.

There was one girl I do remember, he said after taking some time to think about it. Rachel something or other. Davenport, he remembered. Her name was Rachel Davenport.

Go on, said his father.

She was a bit of a wild one.

She still live around here? Monroe asked.

She did. Her family had a summer home here, not far from the Miller place if I remember correctly.

You know where she is now?

She's dead, said the boy. Killed herself a couple years back. At least that's what I heard.

That didn't happen here, said the sheriff. He looked at Monroe. I'd have remembered it.

The boy shook his head. It was somewhere else. Atlanta, I think.

Anyone else you recall? asked Monroe.

There was one other. Her name is Doris Arnold, but it was Cavanaugh back then. She's still here. Works over at the bank as a teller.

You know if anyone has talked to her? Monroe asked the sheriff.

No, idea, the boy replied.

No sir, said his father. Also, he was talking to me.

Monroe took a sip of his coffee and set it back down. You know anything of the father? he asked.

The Miller girl's?

Yes.

The sheriff shook his head. Not much, he said. Just what little I was able to find since you called. She was adopted, you know.

Yes I know.

He looked again at the boy. What about you? She ever talk about her birth father?

Honestly, this is the first I even heard she was adopted.

That girl, you mentioned. Doris. She works at a bank around here?

The sheriff had called the bank manager and talked to him and when Monroe walked in he stopped and gave the receptionist his name and the girl said someone would be right with him. She walked over to an office and stuck her head in the door and the man behind the desk leaned over and looked at him. He pointed down the hall and said something to the girl. The girl shut his door and walked back to where Monroe stood waiting. Right this way, Sheriff, she said.

She led him to a small conference room and let him in and told him to make himself comfortable. Doris will be right with you. Then she left and shut the door.

A moment later Doris Allen stepped in.

Mrs. Allen, he said. Please sit down.

The girl sat at the end of the table. She looked scared. What's this about? she asked.

Don't worry, nothing's happened, he said. I just had a few questions I wanted to ask you.

Questions bout what?

Anna Miller.

She blew out a breath of air and looked at the ceiling and she looked at him again. You had me scared.

I'm sorry. I didn't mean to. I'm a sheriff investigating her disappearance and that of her son.

I've already talked the police, I don't know where they are.

You've not heard from her?

No I've not.

You two were pretty close.

Were.

You're not anymore?

Not for a long while.

How long?

Long enough that she wouldn't call to tell me where she stole off with her son.

Did you know the boy?

What boy?

Her son.

I knew of him, that's about all.

She'd come here on occasion though, to visit her mother.

If you say so.

You never heard from her any of those times?

No sir.

What about before she got married?

What about it?

Did you see her then?

Couple of times. When she came home from college.

You ever have the opportunity to meet her husband?

Her ex-husband.

Her ex-husband.

I met him. Once. Calling it an opportunity is a stretch though.

You weren't impressed?

She looked at her watch. How long's this going to take? My break's only ten minutes.

You're fine. There's no rush here. You'll still get your regular break too.

Monroe's phone went off and he went to silence it and then he looked down the table at the girl. Do you mind telling me what you didn't like about him?

She shrugged. I don't know exactly. It was more just a feeling I had, I guess. It wasn't that he was unfriendly. He didn't talk much and I wasn't around him that long, but you just got this sense about him that he thought himself better than us. You know what I mean?

I do.

She ever talk about him in private?

Anna?

Yes.

No sir. I never was alone with her, after that.

You didn't talk on the phone?

We did some for a while.

And then?

I guess he didn't like it.

Her husband.

Yes sir.

Do you think she was she afraid of him?

The girl thought about it. I'd say if anything, she was afraid for her little boy.

Why do you say that?

I just do.

Would you like some coffee, water? Monroe asked her. She said water would be fine and he got up and left and came carrying two styrofoam cups of water.

Thank you, she said.

Before, Monroe said, when we were talking about meeting Evan Meade, you said us. He thought himself better than us. Who were you talking about?

Me. My friend Rachel. The three of us hung out together.

With Anna?

Yes sir.

And Rachel's the girl who's since passed away?

Yes sir.

Just wondering, do you know how she died?

I know how, but not why.

She looked away and took a deep breath and she took her hands and laid them in her lap. She looked at Monroe. I suppose you want to know the why.

I'd like that very much.

The two of them, she said, they did everything together. Rachel and Anna.

He waited.

I was kind of like a third wheel, at least I felt like that. I mean they were nice and all, and we did everything together, but because of who they were, of what had happened to them as kids, they sort of felt something of a bond toward one another.

What do you mean?

She looked oddly at him. You don't know?

Know what?

Surely, somebody told you.

Nope, he said. Nobody's told me nothing.

I thought maybe her family told you.

Maybe they did and I just forgot.

You wouldn't have forgotten this, she said. It's a wonder I even knew. It's not something they ever talked about. Sometimes they did, but not with me, only with each other. I'd overhear some of it and started to put two and two together.

I'm listening.

Both of them, they were sexually abused. As children, I mean. That's why, or at least I think that's why Rachel killed herself. I can't say for say sure. But I wouldn't blame either one of them if what happened to them was true.

Do you know who was her abuser?

I don't.

She ever lead you to believe it was her father?

Mr. Miller?

Not her step-father. Her biological father.

No sir. I don't think it was him.

Why not?

She talked about him sometimes. Not often, but sometimes.

What'd she say about him?

Not much. Just that she'd wished he'd been around more.

She ever tell you his name?

Why do you ask?

Just wondering. It's just something missing from the puzzle.

It was Caesar, she said. Like the Roman Emperor.

He was seated back in the rental car when he remembered the phone call and took out his phone and looked at it. It was the office. He called it back. What is it? he asked Jeannie when she answered the phone.

It's your father, she said.

What's happened?

Sheriff, he's missing.

Missing where?

Know one knows where. One minute he was sitting with everyone else in the lounge eating breakfast and the next minute he was gone.

Just like that?

Apparently so.

Is that the last anyone saw of him, at breakfast?

I think so.

Monroe looked at his watch. He started the engine. Jeannie?

Yes Sheriff.

What's the weather like up there?

Sheriff, it's goddamn raining cats and dogs.

-Evan Meade

He left Eden Hill just after seven in the morning and three hours later when he walked into the office in Durham, Demski and one other person were already seated in the conference room. He joined them.

Mr. Meade, Demski said, this is Gayle Lanier. She serves as the firm's legal counsel and is an expert in parental-kidnapping issues. She'll be assisting us with your son's retrieval.

The two shook hands. Evan sat down across from her.

First things first, Demski said, referring to his notes, is the custody order. Gayle has spoken with your attorney and she's satisfied that all necessary modifications of the existing order have been taken care of, to mean it now includes the terms of the Hague Abduction Convention and revokes your ex-wife's visiting rights.

The attorney nodded. Though, because she was already in violation of the prior order, she said, an amendment wasn't necessary. Mr. Clegg thought however it might serve as a preventive measure to safeguard against the possibility of a reabduction.

You mean in the case she takes him again?

Yes sir.

Won't she be in jail?

The attorney glanced at Demski and then looked at Evan. For now, she said, no criminal charges, other than those under the Fugitive Felon Act, have been filed, and honestly it's best that they aren't.

Why?

Well, for a couple of reasons. First, your wife has left the country. Of that everyone seems convinced. Some foreign judges have refused to order a child's return under Convention if the parent's return would likely result in their arrest. Second, an outstanding warrant for her arrest and the likelihood of serving jail time will certainly not encourage a voluntary or negotiated return, and finally, if she catches wind of it, it might even push your ex-wife deeper into hiding.

But she will be arrested? Evan looked at Demski.

She would if the FBI found her. But our first priority, you'll remember, is bringing your son home.

And then what happens to her?

That will be up to you and a prosecutor, the attorney answered. And also to her. From what it sounds like to me, she'll probably come back on her own to face whatever civil action she is to face for taking him, but she'll come back regardless just to be close to him. That will be her only chance to have any kind of relationship with her child.

And what of the federal fugitive charge?

It will be dropped. Any criminal prosecution will be brought under state law.

Evan was quiet.

Demski and the attorney shared a look. The woman looked at Evan. You should understand, she said, even in a felony criminal charge, the judge has a choice whether or not to incarcerate a convicted offender. More likely, depending on the circumstances, the sentence is probation. I imagine that's how it will pan out for your ex-wife.

So she just gets away with it?

Probation is not the same as getting away. Nor is turning her son over to his father. She obviously loves him very much. I understand this has been hard on you, and no one is saying you shouldn't seek legal action against your ex-wife, but you have to think what effect it will have on your son, too. Having his mother in jail may not be serving his best interest. There are civil actions you can pursue if you're concerned about vindication or worried about her taking him again.

I'm not worried about this happening ever again.

I understand.

I don't know that you do.

If I could, Demski interjected, to keep us on track, let's focus on finding the youngster first, shall we?

You're aware of the hurricane that struck Georgia? Evan asked him.

I am.

Anna will try to make contact with her mother.

What makes you say that?

Because I know her.

Are you suggesting we go down there and stake out the house?

Evan didn't answer.

We don't have the manpower for that, Mr. Meade. I'm sorry if you thought that's what you were getting. We prefer a more technological approach.

What if it will lead us to her?

I appreciate that you have such a strong conviction about that, but I'm afraid I need to do this my way.

So I have no say?

That's not at all what I'm suggesting.

What then if we disagree?

Mr. Meade, you're not paying me to agree with you. You're paying me to find your son, which I and my colleagues are working very hard to do. The best advice I can give you at the moment is to just sit tight until you hear something further from me.

-Anna

It was still dark when she awoke in the house and the smell of oil and leather assaulted her senses. Her stomach lurched and she flung the covers back just as she felt it rising in her throat. She clamped her hand over her mouth and yanked open the door and hurried down the hall to the bathroom where there just was enough light to see as she jerked open the lid to the toilet and parting the hair from her face bent over the bowl and vomited. Afterwards she wiped her mouth with the hand towel her grandmother kept by the sink. Then she lowered herself to the floor and leaned against the wall.

A long viscid string of spit-vomit had gotten on her nightgown and feeling she might get sick again she pulled the garment over her head and tossed it at the bathtub and sat against the cold porcelain of the tub in just her bra and white panties.

Mommy, are you all right?

She looked up at the door where Oliver stood rubbing his eyes. Behind him was her grandmother. I'm fine, she said and leaned her head back and closed her eyes. I just got a little sick.

Did you throw up? he asked.

She didn't look at him or answer.

Her grandmother shuffled past Oliver and flicked the switch on the bathroom wall and opened one of the cabinets and handed Anna a larger towel and then she turned and walked Oliver back to the bedroom. You could hear her putting him back to bed, speaking softly to him in Italian. He kept asking, What's wrong with Mommy? Why's she sick?

Anna felt her stomach rising again and she lurched forward on her knees and gripped the rim of the bowl and waited for it to come but nothing did and so after the feeling passed she sat back down on the floor and leaned her weight against the wall. She curled her feet beneath her.

When her grandmother came back in she wet a washcloth in the sink and handed it to her. Hai finito?

Anna held the cloth to her face. Her skin was shivering and she reached for the towel which had fallen to the floor and her grandmother picked it up and draped it across her chest and shoulders. Then she left and came back and handed her a thin robe, one of her old ones.

Anna sat there a while and after she'd started to feel better she got up and went to check on Oliver. He'd gone back to sleep. She pulled another blanket from the foot of the bed and tucked it around his shoulders. She kissed him on the forehead and went back to the hall. There was a light on in the kitchen. She found her grandmother standing over the stove boiling a pot of water. Anna came up alongside her.

Tutto bene? Nonna asked.

Anna nodded. Che ora? she asked.

Her grandmother squinted at the clock on the stove. È l'una, she said.

Torni a letto, Nonna.

Starò con te.

Non è necessario. Mi sento bene.

Voglio.

So her grandmother stayed up and sat with her. They drank hot tea while Anna told her about her divorce from Evan and about taking Oliver and fleeing the United States and she told it was not even safe for her to come there because people were searching for them. Her coming there could bring trouble.

La polizia?

Si, Nonna. La polizia. Giudici. Carcere.

Carcere?

Si. Lo porteranno via da me e mi butteranno in prigione.

A la la, Nonna replied. Come? Lui è tuo figlio.

Non importa.

Her grandmother ran her hands across the table cloth and smoothed it out. She scratched at a spot on the table cloth. Something dried and caked on.

La polizia è venuto qui, she said.

Mi dispiace, Nonna.

Her grandmother looked at her and her eyes flared, her skin flushed red in the lamplight. Non dispiaciuta, she said. Tutti pensano che io sono vecchia e senile. Ma posso badare a me stessa.

Nessuno dice che, Nonna.

Che fanno.

Anna was quiet and the old woman reached out and touched her on the hand. When Anna looked at her she tapped her finger against her own temple.

Non ho detto niente. Non ha te. Non sui di lui.

Grazie, Nonna.

They finished their tea and the story and afterwards her grandmother went back to bed and left Anna alone in the kitchen. She stood and went to the phone and picked it up and dialed a number. She waited for the call to go through and looked out the kitchen window into the tiny back yard.

It was dark and cold and quiet. A small four legged shape crossed along the small rock wall that separated her house from the others until it came to a corner and then with a leap disappeared from sight.

A voice answered.

Alfredo? she said. It's me. Anna.

Anna?

I'm sorry, she said. I know I'm not supposed to call.

Is everything OK? Has something happened?

Yes, we're fine.

Where are you? My colleague in Florence called yesterday. Your principal is concerned.

He called you?

Not the principal. My colleague. Your principal spoke to him. He told him he's not seen you in a couple of days. He mentioned Oliver had been sick.

He was. It was nothing. He's better now.

Then where are you?

I'm at Nonna's.

He didn't respond.

I needed to hear some news of my mother, she explained.

Your mother's fine, he said. I spoke to her myself. The danger has passed. Who else have you seen there?

No one else.

You shouldn't have gone, Anna. You know the danger.

Yes I know.

And now you must leave.

I will.

No immediately. Not eventually. Now. You need to get Oliver and your things together and get out of there this morning, before anyone stops by to check on her.

You think someone will?

You've spoken with her, yes?

She didn't answer.

Then you know.

What do I tell Nonna?

Tell her anything. She won't remember.

She will. I can't just leave. What if she tells others?

Hopefully they will think she's remembering something from long ago.

I just couldn't sit there, waiting, Alfredo.

I know. I should have tried myself to reach you. I'm sorry. I wasn't thinking.

She gazed out into the darkness and did not speak. In the distance she heard the sound of a car door closing. She stepped out from in front of the window.

Promise me, Alfredo said, you'll be on that first train leaving San Salvatore. You cannot stay there, Anna. It's not safe. You'll risk everything.

Who would tell? she asked.

There are those who would, you know that. Old grudges. If someone were to ask, they would say they've seen you.

There came a sound then from the front of the house and Anna pulled the phone from her ear and listened. Just a moment, she said to him and she laid the phone down.

Anna? his voice called. Anna?

She came slowly around the table and walked over to the doorway and stopped and stood looking into the living room. There standing at the front door, dressed much the way she had imagined him all these years, in fisherman's garb, was her father.

-Monroe

They had found him a few miles from the old farm trudging slowly in a daze alongside the road. He was wet and lost and though he was wearing a workshirt and a pair of cotton canvas pants, he was shivering beneath his clothes. The officer who had found him had served as a young deputy under his command and knew him well and he understood also the crotchetiness and short-temper that comes with old age because he too had watched his own parents suffer and die from dementia and so when he stopped his cruiser and got out and approached the old man, he did not at once suggest that he get in the car so that he could be driven to the hospital. He offered him a jacket and gave him a wool cap to wear and then he walked with him.

He listened then as the old man talked of his farm and of growing up there with his mother and father and with his two sisters and he talked about how after a summer rain, like the one they were having now, was the best time to catch frogs from the pond.

Just after dusk, the old man told him. For some reason they like it when the water has risen and the banks have flooded. The breeding season has passed and the weather draws them from their burrows to forage.

There fish in there too? the officer asked him.

The old man glanced sidelong at him. Like you wouldn't believe.

And then they talked about fishing and of their favorite spots to find trout and though they had not gone far nor had their conversation lasted long when it came to time to walk back to the car the old man was ready.

Monroe watched him where he lay sleeping in the hospital bed. Carolyn was there too, and Rebecca. There was no one else, not anyone else that was family anyway.

The doctor who had examined him said that he expected a full physical recovery, from the exposure, at least. He hadn't been out that long, only a handful of hours, and the human body could surprise you. It was his mind that most concerned him.

There's no official stage of progression for losing one's mind, the doctor said. Some say three, some seven. What is known is that it starts gradually and then at some point it picks up steam. Eventually the body follows the mind on its downward spiral. I would say we are somewhere in the middle.

But the frogs and the pond, fishing for trout? He remembers those things. He remembers the farm. He was just out talking to people he knew from ages ago.

Yes, that's not uncommon. But you should expect to see more and more changes in his personality and a deterioration of his mental capacity. At some point he will lose his ability to live as he does even now, in assisted living. Sense of balance, appetite, his ability to clean and take care of himself. All of these are possibilities for what awaits down the road. We just don't know. It's time now though to start thinking about what will happen when he becomes solely dependent on someone else for the remainder of his life.

After he'd left, Carolyn touched Monroe on the shoulder to console him. Why don't you go home and get some rest, she said. It's late and you must be tired. You've driven all day to get here.

He looked at his father. Who will stay with him?

I will, said Rebecca.

He looked at her and he looked away at the reflection of them in the window and she said it again. I will stay with Grandpa. I want to be here when he wakes up.

You don't have to do that, he said.

I want to, she said and then she was crying.

I want to, too, said Carolyn.

Monroe turned from the window and he looked at them. Then we'll wait together.

Later, after he'd woken and spoken to them and grumbled about getting something to eat, they all three left, saying they'd be back to visit the next day, and then Monroe parted from Rebecca and Carolyn and he drove to the office and parked out front and went inside. He flipped on the lights and went and sat down at his desk. There were two phone messages for him. One was from the reporter, Jerry Barber, asking about the status of his FOIA request, and the other was from the private investigator Carl Demski.

Monroe looked at his watch. He reached for the phone.

This is Sheriff Rossi, he said. You're message said to call when I got this.

Yes, Sheriff, thank you for getting back with me.

I don't normally return calls this late at night.

I understand. That's fine. I won't take long. In the spirit of cooperation I wanted to share something with you from the State Department.

All right. I'm listening.

It's called a welfare and whereabouts request. It's filed abroad by the Department of Consular Services. They're a kind of federal clearinghouse for international social services. They conduct checks on children of US citizenry living overseas.

Based on what?

On just about anything. In fact, anyone can file this kind of request. Neighbors. Nannies. Clergymen. Teachers. It works pretty much the same as it does in the States.

Clergymen, you say?

Yes, even them. Anyway, my contact at the State Department has provided us with a list of the names of recently filed international welfare requests.

Go on.

Well, none, as you might imagine, list Anna Miller, but there are a number that suggest the possibility that someone somewhere has raised a red flag in regards to her and her son.

Why would you think that?

People who are in hiding behave in strange ways, Sheriff. You know that as well as I do.

And so you're thinking that some good citizen somewhere in this big world is going to report on that strange behavior. Sounds like a bit of a long shot.

It is. Which is the other reason I called you.

You want me to look at the list?

Yes sir.

How many names?

Not many. A handful. Less than a dozen in the last six months, and only half of those appear to be female. There's only one of those with the first name Anna, and that one is living in Italy.

What's the last name?

Caruso.

Monroe sat quietly. After he'd thought about it some he said, Send me the list, Mr. Demski. Not sure I can be of much help, but I'll have a look at it just the same.

-Anna

He asked me not to tell you, Alfredo said. He was sitting across from her at the kitchen table. He'd come right away after their phone call. Her father was there, too, listening and watching and sometimes helping her grandmother and Oliver prepare breakfast.

Why?

I don't know, Anna. He was afraid, or embarrassed.

But you knew he was here?

No, not this time. He lives along the coast. He only comes here occasionally.

Non pensavo, said Caesar, che avresti voluto vedermi.

He didn't think you would want to see him, said Alfredo.

I know what he's saying, Anna barked back. What I don't understand is why you didn't tell me you knew where he was. He's my father.

I don't know why, he said. It never came up and—

It never came up? He abandoned me.

Non era giusto, said Caesar. Avrei dovuto stare per te.

Per me? Avresti dovuto stare per te stesso. Non mi amavi?

Sempre, he nodded. Always.

Avevo bisogno di te.

Si, he answered. Lo so. Mi dispiace.

She watched him. She looked at her uncle. Why does he come here? she asked.

I don't know. Alfredo looked over at Nonna. For the same reason I stayed close to her, I guess. She makes him feel he has a home here still.

Unlike everyone else.

Yes. I suppose.

Anna sat sulking and not speaking. Caesar stood and offered to get her a coffee.

I don't want coffee, she said. He stood looking at her. Non voglio caffè.

Her father nodded solemnly and he walked over to the counter to fix himself some.

Does he know why I'm here? she asked Alfredo.

About your mother?

No, not about her. He doesn't care about her. About me.

He knows that you have come to Italy to be with your son.

But not why?

No. I have not told him why.

You mean he's not asked.

However you'd like to look at it, Anna.

There's no way of looking at it, Alfredo. There only is the truth and then lies.

Then no, he didn't ask why.

She looked away. So what now? What am I supposed to do?

You should do what I asked you to do hours ago.

Just leave?

Yes. It's not safe here. You know that.

What about him? She looked at her father.

I will talk to him.

Will I see him again?

Alfredo did not answer and she did not ask about it again.

After they finished breakfast, Anna and Oliver collected their things and left San Salvatore. The train ride home was long and torturous, what with Oliver still weary and disagreeable from the previous day's journey. It was with great relief when she finally settled him into his own bed late that night.

She could not sleep afterwards and sat on the sofa in the dark staring out the windows into the darker night. When she woke she was lying there still and it was morning and Oliver was asleep in his bed. She got up and made coffee and found when she opened the refrigerator they were out of milk, so she hurried downstairs to pick up a quart before Oliver woke. Giovanni saw her and waved her over but she pretended not to see him and she went back inside and up the stairs to her apartment.

At some point in the day that followed, she was laying with Oliver in his bed reading a book when someone knocked on their door. He wanted to go and answer it but she stopped him.

Don't you want to see who it is? he asked.

It doesn't matter, she answered and then, ashamed by the callousness in her reply, she suggested they wait a while and a bit later they would go out for some ice cream.

Whoever it was at the door left and the day went on without interruption. It wasn't until they were crawling into bed that evening that Oliver even remembered the ice cream.

Tomorrow, she said and the next morning they got up and they both agreed as they were getting dressed that it felt good finally, and for a change, to be getting back to school.

-Evan Meade

When Evan pulled into a gas station outside of Beaufort it was just after four in the afternoon. He filled up the tank and went inside. There was a woman ahead of him in line and he waited and when he stepped up to the counter he asked the clerk did he have a telephone book he could look at. The man reached under the counter and handed him a ragged dog-eared one.

He stepped aside and thumbed through the thin pages until he found the name and he studied the address a moment and tried to picture her street and the house again in his mind. He looked at the clerk.

Do you sell maps? he asked.

The man pointed to a wire rack. Evan selected one and paid the clerk and walked back to his car. He sat down and spread it open in front of him and within a few minutes of searching he found East Street. He folded the map and set it aside and followed Highway 21 toward the waterfront.

He came to the historic district and the layout of the area started to come back to him and he remembered the rest of the way on his own without the help of the map. When he came to her street he turned slowly down it and stopped. If his memory was correct, her house was on the right, three up from where he was parked. He looked at his watch. It was quarter of five. He sat thinking.

He turned around in a driveway and drove back to the main road and over to the waterfront where he parked next to the marina. He got out of the car and strolled along a brick path running the length of the seawall beneath a long stretch of palms until he came to an outdoor dining area where he sat and watched the sailboats and fishing trawlers pass through the tall iron swing bridge over the river and out along the rust-colored salt marshes.

When dark fell he ate dinner at a diner downtown where all around him the talk was of the hurricane and of the recovery. Afterwards he drove around, parking here and there, walking through the Wal Mart, a bookstore, mostly bored, but not staying in any one place for very long.

At midnight he returned to the house on East street. The street was lit and he left the car parked at a small office complex a few blocks away and he took the sidewalk up to the house. He encountered no one else. He stopped out front and bent down to tie his shoe and listened but there was no sound to hear. It was still and quiet and dark. The tall oaks stretched out over the street and along the sidewalk and he stood up straight and walked past the mailbox and came up to the porch and started up.

A dog growled nearby and he stopped. He looked for the animal but it was too dark and he could not see anything. He waited a few seconds then took a step forward and when he didn't hear anything more of the animal he came the rest of the way up the steps.

He worked quickly. The door was locked and so were both windows and he stood then with his hands on his hips thinking, but only for a second because he heard across the street and two houses down a garage door open. He crouched and peered between the rails of the porch as a pair of headlights crept slowly down the drive and into the street. Once the car pulled out of sight he climbed over the porch rail and dropped silently to the ground. Crouching he came around the back of the house where he remembered there'd been a deck. He stopped. The deck was gone. In its place was the frame and partial flooring. There were few tall trees here and the moonlight peeked through the branches and he could see various construction materials and debris covering the ground. Boards. Boxes of deck screws. Extension ladders.

He looked for but found no steps and so searched around for something he might use as a step to lift himself up. Near the corner next to the house he discovered a small stack of concrete blocks and he carried them one by one over to where the door was and he stacked them one on top of the other until he could hoist himself up onto the frame. He kept his body low. Only after he had found his balance did he slowly stand erect. He took his time and scooted his feet as close to the door as the wooden frame allowed. Then reached across the narrow gap and tried the knob. It turned. Slowly he nudged the door open.

Inside the house it was quiet. There was no sound whatsoever and what light there was filtered in through the window over the sink. He knew the floor plan well enough though and had committed it to paper days ago. So he crept around the small kitchen table and past the refrigerator and down the hall and he paused only but a second or two when the floor creaked beneath his weight and as he climbed the stairs his heart began racing. All he could think of was getting to her before something went wrong.

Beneath his weight the floor groaned again but he didn't much worry about that as everything was clear to him and all the answers he'd wanted were almost at his fingertips. So up the stairs he went, taking them two at a time, and when he reached the top of the landing he turned and caught just the shadowy glimpse of some object arcing through the air the instant before it slammed into his stomach.

His lungs emptied and he slammed against the wall. He gripped his mid-section with both hands and gasped for breath. He looked up at his assailant, but there the bat was arcing again and he had just enough time to raise his arms to defend the oncoming blow. The bat glanced off his forearm and it slid to the floor and he saw the old woman in her nightgown holding the bat in her hands and she looked at him with fear in her eyes and then she grunted and raised it to strike him again. He lunged forward and threw his shoulder and all of his weight into the center of her chest. Her arms collapsed around his shoulders and they crashed as one into the wall. He twisted and reached for the bat and he stepped back and glared at her and cursed but the woman denied him his satisfaction and turned and scooted off down the hall.

Evan watched her go, unable to move. He slumped over the bat and gasped for air, his lungs heaving as if at any moment they might explode. He heard a door slam shut at the end of the hall and he looked up and got his feet under him and stood. Anger filled his veins. He raised the bat and charged down the hall and struck at it with every ounce of energy until the frame shattered around the hinges and the door splintered open and he stumbled forward into the room. He found his footing and stopped and looked for her.

She was standing hunched over in the corner, a phone clutched in her hand. He rushed forward and shoved her but still the fight had not left her and she clawed at him and he grabbed her by the arms and spun her and she stumbled backwards over the bed. She lay still then on her back, breathing hard. The phone lay on the floor. He threw her a sidelong glance as he leaned over and picked it up and held it to his ear. He set it down on the nightstand and just stood there then catching his breath. After a while he looked at her.

Get out of my house, she said. She had slid off the bed and was sitting on the floor with her back up against it.

Evan lowered himself to the floor. The bat lay across his knees. He did a quick inventory of his injuries and wondered had she not broken some ribs.

Not till I get what I want, he said.

I don't know where she is.

I think you do. He used the bat as a prop and lifted himself to his feet.

Then you're crazy as hell.

Evan gathered his strength and swung the bat and it struck the nightstand lamp and the lamp shattered into chunks of ceramic and metal and electrical chord. Elena screamed and buried her face in the mattress. Evan turned slowly away, a gradual pain radiating out of his side and spilling over the entire left half of his abdomen. He bit the side of his jaw to keep from wincing. He stood in front of her and held the bat in his hand.

Where is she?

Still she did not look at him. I don't know, she said.

Evan raised the bat again and slammed it into the wall. Picture frames fell from their hooks. The house itself seemed to shudder. The woman screamed and she scrambled to her feet and flung herself onto the bed and over the other side. Evan walked around the end of it and looked at where she lay on the floor.

Where is she? he asked again.

I told you I don't know. There was blood in the corner of her mouth.

He lifted the bat again and spun and smashed into the mirror hanging over her dresser and sent chards of glass flying every which way.

The woman kicked her legs and she scooted across the floor and into the corner where she ran into a small woven basket containing yarn and knitting needles. She cowered. A small, yet not insignificant target. One side of her face was turned to the wall, her hand raised, shielding the other.

Evan tossed the bat on the bed and walked over to her. He said in as calm a voice as he could, I just want my son, that's all.

She had curled herself into a ball, two thin, graying, bare legs protruding from beneath her white night gown. He watched her. I can't help you, she said.

Evan looked away. He looked at the damage he'd done to the room. He noticed something partially hidden under the corner of the bed. One of the framed photos he'd knocked either from the nightstand or the wall. He leaned over and picked it up. It was a photo of Anna and Oliver. He studied the photograph and thought it looked recent, in the last six months, he thought. The two of them were sitting together on a park bench amongst tall trees and in the distance, barely a part of the frame, stood a statue set in what appeared to be a large ornate pond. Oliver was wearing a ship captain's hat and though Anna's hair was the same length, it was dyed a different color.

This is your last chance, he said. He turned to look at her and when he did he saw out of the corner of his eye her arm dart out from her side and swing towards him. Something metallic flashed in the light as she brought her arm down and he felt it pierce his foot. Searing hot pain shot up his leg and he looked down at the floor and saw protruding from the top of his shoe the curved end of a lime green knitting needle. Evan wailed as the woman clambered on hands and knees for the door.

He bent down and gripped the end of the needle and drew it slowly from his foot. It made a plucking sound as it came free and he dropped it to the floor. He gripped his foot with both hands and gritted his teeth. He could hear her running down the hall now. He lifted his injured foot and lurched for the door. When he came to the hall he saw at the other end the woman climbing to her feet. She headed down the stairs and he went after her.

He stopped when he came to the first floor landing and listened, wary of another attack, and slowly he turned toward the back of the house. She was there at the end of the long hallway standing in the kitchen doorway. She held the wall phone in her hands. He ignored the pain in his foot and ran toward her. She looked at him frantically and holding the phone to her ear managed to scream, Help me. Help me.

He crashed into her and the phone flew from her hands. She was thrown across the kitchen and landed hard against the back door.

You just wouldn't listen, he growled at her. Goddamn you women.

Elena got to her feet but her back was pressed against the door and there was no where for her to go. She slid her hands behind her.

Evan stepped forward. I'm not leaving here without you giving me something.

I've told you already. Go to hell.

They locked eyes for a few seconds and then he charged her. She braced for collision but then something happened and her hand found the handle to the door and she grasped it and turned and it fell open behind her. She held there briefly in the doorway, like some cartoonish caricature of herself and then her footing failed her and she fell backwards, her arms flailing at the air, her eyes rolled back too, her head turned, searching for what lurked in the gloom behind her.

Evan stood watching her and he walked up to the door and looked down at where she lay on the ground, twisted and irregular, her head resting on the short stack of concrete blocks that he had erected himself to gain his illegal entry.

-Monroe

Monroe sat on the edge of the sofa bouncing his knee and flipping through a travel magazine. Pictures of exotic beaches. Lean, handsome men. Beautiful, young women in bikini bathing suits. Big white luxurious yachts. She'd handed him the magazine when they got to her house and told him to make himself comfortable. I'll be back in a jiffy, she'd said.

His stomach growled and he looked at his watch. He kept glancing for her to come back down the hall.

An hour earlier, he had stopped by the library just as it was closing to ask for Grace's help with the information Demski had sent him from the State Department. But instead of talking about it he had talked about his father and of Rebecca and his ex-wife and afterwards she had looked at him sadly and asked when the last time he'd enjoyed a home cooked meal. He said to her, No idea.

Come on, she told him.

Where are we going?

To my house?

Your house?

Yes. Do you know how to get there?

He looked at her but didn't answer.

Here's the thing, she said, looking him directly in the eyes. I've got a pot of meat and potato stew that's been cooking in the crock pot since noon. You've had a horrible week and I'd like to do something nice for you. Is that all right?

He nodded. Sure, he said. He shrugged. Of course. I'd like that.

He sat listening for her and looking at the pictures and occasionally wondering of the Blazer parked out in the drive in front of her house. He was about to get up and ask could he move it around to the back when Grace stepped into the hallway entrance in her bare feet and wearing a short gray sweater dress that hung loose around the collar.

Monroe closed the magazine. He looked at where she was standing with one hand resting on the door jam and her one hip dropped and the knee bent and he could see the outlines of her breasts and the hard prominence of her nipples and when he looked at her in the face he saw she was watching him too. He rose to his feet and set the magazine down on the stack of others on the coffee table.

Anything good in there? Grace asked.

Only things a sheriff can't afford.

That's the point of it, isn't it? Tease you with things you can't have. Make you feel like you're always wanting for something? Just once it'd be nice for someone to show you the things you can have.

He looked at her and she smiled. She arched her eyebrows. Hungry? she asked.

Monroe followed her into the kitchen. Her feet made little tapping noises on the tiled floor and he walked over to where a crock pot sat on the counter and he cracked the lid and peered in.

Didn't believe me, did you? she said.

He set the lid back on the pot and turned and looked at her. She was stretching up on her toes to reach into an opened cabinet for two wine glasses, her skirt riding up her thigh, and she set them down and asked did he prefer red or white.

Either is fine, he answered.

When she left he turned and looked out the window over the sink toward the front yard and the street beyond. All he could see though was the dark and his own reflection looking back him.

Everything okay? she asked.

He turned. It's fine, he said.

She was holding a bottle of red wine. She glanced toward the window and then looked at him. If you're worried about someone coming by, seeing your car or whatever.

He stopped her. It's okay, he said. He reached over and took the bottle of wine and turned to face the cabinets. Where might I find a corkscrew?

She got it for him and he opened the bottle while she tasted and then adjusted the seasoning of the stew. When she finished he handed her the glass of wine and she took it and set it aside on the counter next to his. Do you mind if I do something first? she asked.

Not at all.

She stepped closer and kissed him on the mouth and he put his arms around her and he caressed her shoulder and brushed the hair away from her face and she moaned and kissed him harder. They pressed up against one another. He reached down and felt for the hem of her dress but she stopped him. She took his hand and led him back through the house to the bedroom where she made him sit down on the bed. She turned off the bedside lamp and went into the bathroom and shut the door and when she came out again she was not wearing anything and he looked at her hips and the smooth shape of them bathed from behind by the orange-yellow glow of a candle burning somewhere in the bath. She came forward and took his hand in hers and pulled him up from the bed.

It's your turn now, sailor-man, she said as she reached for his belt.

Later that evening, after they'd eaten and he'd helped her clean up the kitchen she reminded him of the work he'd brought with him to the library for her to help with. He went out to the Blazer and got the file folder with the information from Demski had sent him and he carried it back to the house. He laid it on the table, but as he was sitting down to it, his mobile phone rang. He answered it.

Sheriff Rossi?

This is him.

Sheriff, this is Tom Jennings, down in Beaufort. You had breakfast with me and my son the other day.

Yes, I remember. Monroe walked to the door and stepped outside and over to the side yard. What can I do for you, Tom?

Well, I was hoping you might be able to help me out with a little something that's gone on down here.

I can try.

It involves Elena Miller.

Monroe looked over at the kitchen window where he could see Grace busy with something at the sink. Go on, Tom. I'm listening.

A neighbor found her early this afternoon outside her house, under her own back deck. Looks like she might have fallen or been pushed.

Is she all right?

No sir. I'd say she's a long way from all right.

Book IV

-Evan Meade

He parked in the garage and got out of the car wincing and holding his side and he pulled down the garage door and quickly crossed the drive and hurried into the house. Inside it was dark except for the nightlights she liked to keep plugged in at various places along the countertops and walls and he went around one by one pulling these out and when he had finished he went back through the rooms drawing the shades and window blinds.

He fished a small flashlight from a kitchen drawer and walked back to their bedroom and undressed and went and stood in front of the mirror over the bathroom sink to inspect his injured ribs but it was too dark to see anything, even with the small flashlight. It was just a swollen dark purplish splotch.

She nailed you good, he said, feeling tenderly with his fingers along the outer edge of the bruise, grimacing here and there. But you'll live.

He showered and shaved by candlelight and then with the towel still wrapped around him he went to the cabinet where they kept some first aid supplies and he found a roll of elastic adhesive dressing and used it to wrap his midsection and then he sat down on the toilet and did the same with his foot, which was causing him less grief than his ribs.

He went to the closet and turned on the light and shut the door. He looked around at what was left of their things. His dress clothes. Winter jackets. Some shoeboxes and extra blankets. From under the hanging clothes he found the only suitable thing he could use to carry clothes in that Angela hadn't taken. He unzipped the pink sports duffle and stuffed it with a few changes of clothes and got dressed in a pair of nice slacks, a striped button-down and a pair of soft leather loafers. He slung the bag over his shoulder, turned out the light and walked back through the house to the side door. Before opening the door, he looked at his watch. He'd been there for less than an hour.

The day before at about that same time, he'd been driving back to Eden Hill when he and the car he'd been following sped past a State Trooper partially hidden in the median. The trooper pulled out behind them, flashing on his blue lights. Evan saw them and cursed and he slowed and his heart began to hammer in his chest, his side began to throb. He pulled to the shoulder. But the cruiser blew by him in pursuit of the other driver and Evan just sat there a moment or two collecting himself and his thoughts. When he pulled back onto the interstate he drove to the next exit and turned around and doubled back thirty miles to a Red Roof Inn he had passed. He spent the day there watching the television and nursing his aching ribcage and tending to the puncture hole in his foot where she'd stabbed him. With no supplies, he left them both much as they were, except for a soak in a bath of hot water and then keeping them elevated.

A short while after noon, he called Carl Demski. I have a
photograph, he said.

A photograph of what?

Of them, Evan said.

Is it recent?

I think so. Her hair is different.

Can I ask how you came into possession of it?

Evan didn't answer.

Mr. Meade?

I'm here.

Does this photo reveal something useful?

It proves I was right.

Right about what?

Everything.

He drove alone through the flashing yellow signal lights
and empty intersections and as he left the city limits and
entered the rural highway he remembered traveling these
very same roads, also at night, searching for them six
months earlier. He hadn't been sure then what he was
looking for, a sign of something. A broken down car. A
traffic accident. Something other than what he'd found:
them gone. As if finding them injured or dead on the side of
the road were in some way better.

That's what he'd expected anyway, and even now his
eyes were drawn to the obscured edge of the headlight
beams where the road slipped away into oblivion for sign of
a wrecked vehicle, as if the tall loblolly pine forest and thick
scrub oak underbrush might just now be offering them up
for his discovery.

He thought of all those squandered miles. Reporting them missing. Searching for them. No one taking him seriously until it was too late. Six months of torment. Of course there had been no accident. She was not in some ditch somewhere. Her car had been found in Richmond. She'd taken a bus to Cincinnati. Then she'd quietly slipped into hiding. But her secret was about to end.

-Monroe

Monroe sat at the edge of his desk talking through with Clarence what he knew about the assault against Elena Miller. Mostly he was just thinking, hypothesizing the way lawmen do, and waiting for the phone to ring.

You think the father had anything to do with it? the deputy asked from where he was leaning in the doorway.

I don't know.

It sure doesn't sound like something a banker would have in him to do, does it? Beating up old ladies?

Monroe glanced at him. You are forgetting something. The alleged kidnapper, his ex-wife, was a school teacher.

Clarence shrugged. I reckon, he said. It'd sure go to show there's a bit of darkness in all of us.

Tell me something I don't know.

Jeannie excused herself past Clarence and stepped in carrying a coffee cup and she handed it to Monroe. Anything from Beaufort? he asked.

I'd have told you if there was, she answered and left.

Monroe carried the coffee and walked around the desk and sat down in the swivel chair. He took a sip and looked back across the desk at Clarence. I hate to ask this, he said, but the Blazer needs filling. I should have done it last night. Would you mind?

You want me to bring it around then?

Just gas it for now.

The deputy left and Monroe sat drinking his coffee. He called out and asked Jeannie if she'd seen the file he'd had with him from the day before.

She appeared at his door. You had it last night when you left, she said. I believe you were headed to the library.

Monroe thanked her and was reaching for the phone when the office door opened. Jeannie turned to look who it was had come in. She said, Here it is now I believe.

Monroe leaned over and looked past her through the doorway and saw Grace approaching the counter. He hung up the phone and got up and came out of his office to meet her. She handed him a file folder. You left this, she said. She glanced over at Jeannie and her mouth curled into a quick smile. I hope you don't mind, she said to Monroe, I took a minute and looked through it.

Not at all, Monroe said. You'll remember that's why I stopped by.

I remember, she replied. Her lips twitched and she looked again at Jeannie who was watching her with curiosity. How are you Jeannie? Grace asked.

Just fine, Grace. You?

Very well, thank you much for asking.

Monroe stepped around the counter. Come on back, he said to Grace. You can tell me what you found.

She sat down in his office and crossed her legs. She was wearing a short mini-skirt and Monroe stood staring too long at her bare legs. She cleared her throat and he looked at her and then he sat down and thanked her for bringing the papers to him. I would have come got them, he said.

It's no problem. I was in the area. She looked around his office. Her hair looked redder even than normal. I've never been in a sheriff's office before.

This is just a temporary one. My office is down at the jail, being remodeled.

Is it bigger? she asked.

Way bigger, he responded.

She looked at him and smiled. So?

Monroe watched her. You mentioned you'd taken a look at these papers.

The names. Right. She uncrossed her legs and scooted forward to the edge of her seat in order to reach the desk. So, I took the list you left (at my house), she mouthed, and crossed referenced it against those in my own little database I created. These were just some surnames you'd mentioned before, family names, things like that, except for one.

I know which one.

You do?

Yes.

Which?

Caruso.

Yes, that's the one. How'd you know?

He told her about his conversation with Doris Allen and of his call with Demski explaining the State Department's role in this.

She looked at him oddly. So what did you need from me?

I don't know. I guess I just wanted to share it with you.

It says she's living in Florence, Italy, working as an art teacher at some school. The school's principal generated the wellness check.

I saw that.

That's her, isn't it? Grace said, excited.

He looked at her and he was smiling too.

When he spoke to the private investigator, Carl Demski, who called his office a short while later, he told him about the assault against Elena Miller.

You think he's behind it?

There's a good possibility. If so, how's this change what you're working on?

Change it how?

I don't know. Putting it on hold I guess while it gets straightened out.

I can assure you it won't do that, Sheriff. Unless there's solid proof, we still have a job to do.

And if the father is and he goes to jail?

I suppose if that happens someone will have to decide what to do with his son.

They'd make him a ward of the state most likely. There's no other living family that I know of.

Yes sir.

There was an interruption on the other end of the line. A woman's voice. Demski responding. Monroe listened but couldn't make out their words. When he came back on the phone, Monroe said to him, The courts will likely seize control of his bank accounts. You won't get paid.

We will eventually.

You sound confident of that, Mr. Demski.

I am, Sheriff.

Monroe was quiet a moment. Who else you have working on this?

Who else?

Yes. You mentioned a partner before, the last time we spoke. Said he was already someplace overseas.

Right about now, he's on a train headed to Florence, Italy.

Monroe sat forward. A shadow filled the doorway. He looked up and saw Jeannie standing there, watching him.

All right, Monroe said finally. I trust you will keep me posted.

Yes sir.

Monroe hung up the phone and looked over at Jeannie.

That was the sheriff down in Beaufort, she said. Elena Miller has died.

Monroe sat looking at her, not saying anything in response. He sighed and looked out the little window beside his desk. Then he looked over again at Jeannie. He say anything else?

He asked you to call back when it was convenient.

All right.

You want me to get him back on the line.

Not just yet. And Jeannie?

Yes, Sheriff.

Will you let Clarence know to go ahead and bring the truck around.

-Anna

She'd not been to bed long when a sound woke her. She looked at the numbers of the digital clock and sat up in her bed. Outside it was raining steadily. She was about to lay back down when she heard then the knock at her door. She felt a rush of panic and slid out of the bed and went to the window. She pulled back the curtain and looked out but could distinguish nothing of the street below through the streaks of rain. She slipped on her robe and went down the hall and stopped and stuck her head in Oliver's room and listened for his breathing and then closed his door and walked lightly down the hall trying not to make any sound and when she came to the door she pressed her palms against it and listened. Her hands were shaking.

Anna, a voice hissed. It was Tore.

She opened the door and stepped back and he looked at her but didn't speak as he stepped across the threshold and brushed past her into the room. He was dripping wet.

I'm sorry, he said. I hope I haven't frightened you. But something terrible has happened.

She shut the door and went and got him a towel and handed it to him and while he wiped his face, she asked him to tell her about it.

He sat her down on the sofa and told her about her mother and after she had calmed down she asked how he had found out.

Your uncle. Someone called him. The police, I think. He told Giovanni. He wanted to come tell you, but I insisted.

Her eyes were still wet from crying. She dabbed at them with a tissue. There is only one person, she said, who would do this, who would be willing to hurt her.

Your uncle said as much.

She looked at him. So you know about Evan. What should I do?

I don't know, Tore told her.

She told him then everything. About the kind of person her ex-husband was. About Oliver and her decision last spring to take him. About coming to Florence and of Alfredo's connections and how she had used them to find a job and get Oliver into his school. She told him of the hurricane and of going to her grandmother's and her uncle's warning to leave, and then seeing her father again for the first time in many, many years.

That's a whole other story, she said about that. I'm not even sure what to think. I guess I just wish I'd known.

She looked at him. Isn't that strange, him coming back into my life just as my mother leaves it.

Tore watched her and did not answer.

What would you do? she asked him.

I don't know, he said. You have to decide what's right.

There's probably not much anyone can do at this point anyway. Wait, I guess. I could never just turn myself in.

Do you think he will come here, this Evan?

Yes, she said. If he's found out where I am, he'll come. And he'll want more than just Oliver. He'll want to get even for what I did.

Tore was quiet and after a few seconds he stood and went to the window and looked out into the midnight darkness.

I never thought any of this would happen, she said and she was crying softly again.

He turned and looked at her.

Or maybe I did, she went on. Part of me knew, I guess. She wiped her eyes. But I was only thinking of him. I hope you understand that. I just wanted to be a good mother to him. I was always having to work so hard against everything his father was doing and teaching him. With him, Oliver would never have a chance.

Why doesn't matter, said Tore. You love him. That's what matters.

I do, she said. When I was growing up I never could imagine myself as a mother. I hated my stupid, little life. Why would I want that for anyone else? She rolled her eyes. It sounds so pathetic, when I think about it. Like I'm just complaining.

I don't think that, Tore said.

She looked at him. Just listen, she said. Please.

I was seven when my mother and father divorced, but they had been out of love long before that. My father, that's Alfredo's brother, could not settle down. He was a simple man and liked being on his own and being a husband and father was hard on him. My mother despised him for what she called his lack of ambition. She kicked him out when I was three and he pretty much never came back, only to sign the papers at the divorce. I didn't even get to see him then.

We moved in with my grandmother, the one I just visited, in San Salvatore. There my mother was able to work more than one job and focus on more important things, like making money. She was obsessed with money, so much so that I hardly ever saw her either. My Nonna took care of me.

She taught me to cook, how to clean, how to take care of myself.

Her husband, though, my grandfather was a terrible man. Things happened in that house, terrible things I will never forget. When my mother found out about them she swore to leave Italy and never come back. At that time she was having an affair with a married man, a US soldier about to rotate back to the States, and somehow she convinced him to take the two of us with him. He was a good man, kinder than most I'd known up to that point, and he adopted me and we moved to the US and my sad sorry life became even sorrier. I hated it there. Everything about it. The move, leaving my family. I couldn't speak or understand the language. Everyone looked down on me, especially my classmates. I worked hard to erase any trace of a difference between us, even the accent with which I spoke changed. And even before that, back here in Italy, it was hardly any better. As soon as people learned we were leaving, they seemed to hate us. They already knew everything about my grandfather, they knew about my mother's affair. They thought we were running away from it all, not just leaving.

Anna looked over at Tore. He was looking down at the floor. I'm sorry, she said. I really shouldn't be bothering you with this.

He looked at her and shook his head. No, no, please. It's no bother.

When I finally had a son myself, I learned what it was truly like to love and be loved by another just for who you are. To have that taken away. She looked over at him. I just couldn't let that happen.

I believe you did the right thing, he said.

Thank you, she said. And thank you for listening. I just needed to say it. I needed to tell someone those things.

-Monroe

When Monroe returned the call to the sheriff's office in Beaufort he and Clarence were headed over to the courthouse to get a warrant to search the house. Whoever answered the call told him the sheriff was out of the office and he wouldn't be returning until later. Monroe gave them his name and number and the nature of his call and was put on hold. A second later they patched him through to the sheriff's radio.

I'm always surprised when these things happen, said the sheriff of the woman's death. It's the damndest part of this job. You'd think after twenty years I'd be less shocked by what horrible things people are capable of.

I was just having that same conversation earlier today.

You come to any conclusions about?

Just one. It's people, plain and simple. Some of them get out into the world, around others and they get real clever at living behind a mask.

The lab is still sifting through evidence, but some has turned up. A couple of foot prints. Some droplets of blood. Could be hers, but we don't think so based on her injuries and where the blood was found.

Any idea on who might be responsible?

Not anyone down here. Least I don't think so. Even the bad guys are still busy cleaning up after this mess of a storm. What about your fella up there?

I'm headed there now.

Don't suppose you have something on her next of kin, do you?

Just the daughter, the one missing.

A neighbor here had the number of someone. He lives overseas somewhere. Belgium, I think. Far as I know he's been told. Not sure what he's doing about funeral arrangements.

His name Caruso?

Maybe. That rings a bell. Anyway, I appreciate your help with this, Monroe. I'll be in touch with more later today, I hope.

Monroe hung up with the sheriff and called the city police and asked them to send a car and meet him at the father's address. Then he called the magistrate's office about the warrant. When they arrived at the house and pulled up there were four patrol cars parked in the street and one more in the driveway. A crowd of gawkers stood at the edge of the road. More standing at the house next door. They parked behind one of the city cars and got out and walked up to the house. A uniformed officer greeted him. This way, Sheriff.

They walked up and Monroe looked at the officer standing there and said, I take it he's not here.

No sir.

He looked at the street. I asked for just one car.

The officer shrugged

All right, Monroe said. He nodded toward the house. Show me.

The house was a wreck. Dirty dishes, pots, food stuff everywhere. A smell of something rotting. There was a gaggle of officers standing in the living room amidst the stacks of folded laundry from days before.

Any any idea where the wife is? Monroe asked.

None of them answered.

She's definitely not here, the youngest looking one finally replied.

Have you checked the crawl space?

The officer looked at him. Well, no sir. Not yet.

Better get to it then.

Monroe walked back to the bedrooms. He looked in the closets and opened a few dresser drawers. Any weapons? he asked.

No sir. We've not been over the place top to bottom, but none's turned up so far.

Monroe did a half-circle around the room and came back and stopped in front of the officer. He looked at him. Well, Monroe said, I guess somebody ought to alert the airports.

You think that's where he's headed?

That'd be my first guess, Monroe answered.

-Evan Meade

The first leg of the flight took him to Montreal. It arrived at 4:25 in the afternoon. As the plane approached the gate, Evan looked out the tiny window at the day. It was bright and sunny. Clear blue skies. Beautiful travel weather. He got off the plane and checked through customs carrying the pink duffle bag and he walked to his connecting gate without any trouble. Once there he sat with his back to the busy terminal and watched the planes taxiing down the runway. He did not have to sit there long before a woman's voice came over the intercom announcing that all passengers of his flight could begin boarding.

He gave the attendant his ticket and she smiled at him and said, Have a good flight, and he filed in with the last of the travelers and stowed the bag in the overhead bin and took his seat. The seats were vacant beside him until a beset-looking boy and a girl came trudging down the aisle loaded with backpacks and gift bags. The girl was in front reading the seating row numbers. She stopped in front of him and looked at the two empty seats and then she looked at him. Evan stood and stepped into the aisle. It took them a while to unload themselves of their carry-ons but after they did they sat down.

Evan sat down and buckled his seat belt. The girl was sitting beside him and after she got herself situated she looked over at him and smiled. About didn't make it, did we? she said with a thick British accent.

Evan smiled and tossed his head in a slight nod.

Where're you headed? she asked him.

Paris, he answered. Like you.

Is that your final stop?

No. Then on to Italy.

The girl brightened. Us too! She reached over and felt with her hand for the boy's arm. She rested it there. It's our honeymoon. To what part of Italy are you headed?

Florence.

Oh, Florence is beautiful. You'll love with it. Have you been there before?

He shook his head. Once, he said.

Fantastic. Stephan, my new husband, here, he lived in Florence for a while as a student. Are you traveling there for business or pleasure?

A little of both, he answered.

That's splendid.

One of the flight attendants walked down the aisle closing the overhead doors and telling various passengers to upright their seat backs. Another was passing out earphones. As the plane began backing away from the gate, the girl turned to him and asked if he flew much.

Not really, he said.

I hate flying. Especially these long flights. The sooner you fall asleep the better. Besides, what else is there to do, right? If it weren't for going to distant new places, I'd never even step on an airplane. Strange, considering I became a journalist partly so I could travel.

He nodded and looked straight ahead.

What about you? she said. What sort of work do you do for a living?

Investment banking.

Like for retirement?

Yes. Amongst other things too.

Do you like it?

Mostly, he answered. Some days are better than others.

I imagine so, she said. I don't think I could be trusted with other people's money, especially those who favor it over themselves or their own children. I see you're married. Do you have children?

A son, he said.

How old?

He's five.

I love children. Not sure I could stand having one around me all day, but sooner or later we'll probably give it a go. She glanced over at her young husband who had plugged in earphones and had his head leaned back and eyes closed. She said, He thinks he wants to have a houseful of them, but he's not the one spitting them out, is he? He also thinks if they don't work out there's some way to give them all back. Has he got a rude awakening?

You said he lived in Florence?

A few years back. The girl nudged him and the boy looked at her. He took one of the earbuds out.

This fellow is headed to Florence, she told him, pointing at him with her thumb.

The boy leaned forward and looked at him and nodded and then sat back.

You should tell him about it, the girl prompted.

Actually, Evan said to her. It'd be helpful if he could suggest a hotel.

Of course, she said.

The boy spoke up. He sounded American. What part of the city are you headed? he asked.

Evan bent forward and looked at him. Something around the Boboli Gardens.

Cheap or expensive?

Whichever is closest.

There are dozens, the boy answered without looking at him.

Cheap then.

The boy gave him the name of a hotel right away. But, he said, if you want something really cheap you should stay near the University there is a place that is used mostly by students. It's the cheapest place in town.

Evan said he'd look into it, and after they were airborne he pushed his seat back and closed his eyes and tried to do what the girl suggested and get some sleep.

-Anna

She was waiting for him at the bottom of the steps outside
of his school with a few other parents, mostly mothers,
when a pair of nuns swung open the doors and stepped
outside. A mob of children followed. They swarmed down
the steps past her and behind them the younger class came
out in a more orderly fashion and she spotted Oliver almost
immediately. When he saw her he broke ranks and ran
down the steps smiling. She bent down and hugged him
and asked how was his day.

It was good, he said.

Really?

Ask me how old I am, he said.

All right. How old are you?

No, in Italian.

She looked at him. Quanti anni hai? she asked.

Cinque anni, he said. Now ask me my name?

Come ti chiami?

Mi chiama--

Mi chiamo, she corrected.

Mi chiamo Oliver.

She smiled. Va bene, she said. Molto bene. Il mio piccolo
principe.

Your what?

My little prince, she answered and she hugged him again and they started home.

When they reached the piazza they stopped to get Oliver an ice cream and to say hello to Giovanni but he was busy taking a delivery and so they went on. Outside their building Anna was searching her purse for her keys when a young woman walked up. She said hello and introduced herself as Claire Covington. You are Anna Caruso, I presume?

Who are you?

Claire Covington, the girl repeated. She smiled and handed Anna a business card. From the US Consulate General office, she said. American Citizen Services Unit. The girl glanced down. You must be Oliver.

Oliver licked his ice cream.

The girl smiled and looked again at Anna, who was still reading the card. She asked, Do you have a few minutes we could talk?

Anna looked up. I'm sorry, she said. I don't understand.

Of course not. I apologize. This is my first one of these. It's nothing to worry about. I'm sure we'll get through it. First, though, I should ask: Are you okay with us speaking English? I'm happy to speak Italian if it will make it easier for you to follow.

No, English if fine.

Great! I thought so. So, the girl went on, why am I here? I am here because an official inquiry has been made of the Consulate to conduct a welfare and whereabouts check on you and your son. My job is to assist with that request by asking some very simple questions. It shouldn't take more than a few minutes.

Requested by who? Anna asked.

I'm sorry, the girl said. I can't reveal that information.

What kind of check did you say?

Welfare and whereabouts.

What does that mean?

It means the US government was asked by someone to report on the general well being of you and your son.

On our well being?

That's correct.

Yet you can't tell me who it is who is doing the asking.

No ma'am. I'm afraid I can't.

Then I'm afraid too I can't answer your questions. Anna took Oliver by the hand and started to walk in the opposite direction of their building's entrance.

Your son is a US citizen, correct?

Anna stopped. She turned around. You know the answer to that already.

The girl nodded. This won't go just away, she said apologetically. You should know that. If need be, we can get the local authorities involved, but of course I'd rather we handle this ourselves.

The two women studied one another.

It's just a few questions, the girl said. From what I've seen so far, it really won't take long.

Anna looked down at Oliver and she looked back at the girl and motioned toward the cafe. We'll sit out here, she said.

They crossed the piazza and choose a table and sat down. The girl asked if she would like something to drink. Anna shook her head.

Can I have a water? Oliver asked.

No sweetheart. When we get inside.

It's on me, the girl said. She stood and went inside and when she came out she was carrying three bottles of water. Here you go, she said and set the bottle down in front of the boy. Looks like you could use a napkin or two also. She handed him a stack of those to wipe his face of the ice cream.

Thank you, Anna said.

My pleasure.

The girl leaned over and took from the large bag she had with her a pad of paper and a pen. She opened the pad and began writing. When she raised her eyes again she looked around at the piazza and then at Anna and she asked the name of the place where they were sitting.

Lo Stivale, Anna replied.

The girl wrote that down. She looked up. Okay, she said. She looked at Oliver and then back at Anna. So tell me a little about yourselves.

What would you like to know? Anna asked.

Well, the girl thought about it. How long have you been in Florence?

Since March.

And before Florence, you were living where?

In the US.

Whereabouts in the US?

The girl was poised to write and when Anna didn't respond she glanced up.

I'm sorry, Anna said. Honestly, I don't feel comfortable talking about this with you. I mean, we just met and you gave me your card and all, but...

I understand completely, the girl said. She put her pen down. I do, she said. I really do. If you'd rather, we can go down to the Embassy. I have an office there and you can see that I'm not some kind of weirdo getting her jollies from pestering kind strangers with personal questions.

Anna looked away. She looked back at the girl. We were living in a small suburb of Cincinnati, she said.

Really, I'm from northern Indiana. We used to drive through Cincinnati all the time going to Tennessee to visit my grandparents. Most of the time I was asleep—my Dad would have us leave in the middle of the night—but every now and then I'd catch a glimpse of the stadium, or he'd wake us as we were crossing the bridge to bear witness, his words, to his Big River. That's what he called the Ohio. He loved Johnny Cash. Anyway, I digress. Where were we? Yes, you lived in Cincinnati before coming here in March. And in Florence you are employed as, she paused to look through her notes.

I teach art, Anna said.

Art teacher, right. She wrote that down.

And your son, he goes to school.

Yes, she said and she gave her the name, which she also wrote down.

The girl looked at the boy. When she looked again at Anna she spoke in a slightly softer voice. You and his father, you're not together?

No we are not.

Is he back in Cincinnati?

I don't know where he is. We've not seen him in a while.

I see. So you do not collect any kind of financial support from him?

No we do not.

Is teaching your only source of income?

And my art. I have a booth at one of the markets.

Oh, which one?

Sant' Ambrogio.

I've heard of it. In the Piazza Lorenzo Ghiberti, isn't it?

Yes, Anna nodded.

Are you there every weekend?

Not every, but many.

It is one of the things I love about this city. There is art everywhere. You are so lucky to have a talent for it. I wish I did, but I'm all thumbs when it comes to using my creativity for making things. My time is much better spent analyzing the rate of pick-pocket arrests to gauge the threat to Americans' travel plans.

Anna nodded.

That was a joke, the girl added.

I'm sorry, Anna replied. I'm finding it hard to relax, not knowing why you are here now asking me these questions.

I know.

Why would someone ask for this of us?

Honestly, most of the times it's a parent of a child who's been taken overseas. They just want to know that they are safe and being taken care of.

Is this the case now?

No, she said, it isn't. This call came from here in Florence, not the US.

From here?

Yes. I'm sorry I can't tell who from who.

Anyone can request it though?

She nodded. As long as the person they're asking about is a US citizen, we're obligated to follow up.

The girl closed her notebook and set her pen down. She looked across the small table at Anna. But you seem like a nice person and a good mother, so I'll tell you this much.

Anna waited.

You might want to find another school to teach at.

-Monroe

Monroe was sitting at a table near the back of the diner watching the door when the reporter walked in. He waved his hand in the air and Barber spotted him and headed back. Morning, Sheriff, he said as he sat down. I appreciate you finally agreeing to meet with me.

Well, you've been patient, mostly, and I figured there just never will be a good time for it. Coffee?

Thank you.

Monroe glanced over at the counter and motioned and the waitress came over. He ordered two coffees.

Anything else, Sheriff?

Monroe looked at Barber, who shook his head. That'll be all, Marjorie. Thank you.

She left and Monroe studied the reporter. He was surprised at how much younger he looked when you took the time to look beyond his byline, which for him usually followed some hard, muckraking bit of small town reporting from the mind of someone much older, one whose impression of the world has been turned wholly grim and cynical either from experience or adopted ideology. But his short, whimsical hair, stubbly beard, and plaid blazer suggested the persona of an English professor or fiction writer surveying what is for all the human condition, which is to discover that life is not meaningless and our isolation in this world is not inevitable.

What's on your mind, Mr. Barber? he asked.

The freedom of information request on the Meade abduction.

I have it right here, said Monroe. He slid an envelope across the table to the reporter. Barber looked at it but left it were it was. I hope you understand, he said, I'm just trying to do my job.

I understand completely.

I only want what's best for the citizens of our community.

As do I.

Marjorie brought them their coffee and set them down in front of them. She left and Monroe took a sip from the mug and held it in both hands and he looked across at the reporter. He pointed a finger at the envelope. So let's talk a minute about what's in there, shall we?

All right.

There's only two things that I believe warrant discussion at our little get together. The first you'll find in there. The other I'll get to in a minute. To begin, though, I'd like to go over those three-and-a-half hours you seem to have yourself so charged up about.

It's not just the time.

Monroe held up his hand. You'll get your chance. I promise. But I'm older and so you get to listen to me first. Fair enough.

The reporter nodded. Fair enough.

So Mr. Meade called our office around two-thirty that Sunday. One of my deputies took the call. He took down the complaint that Meade's son had not been brought home pursuant to a court order. As per department protocols, an officer was dispatched to determine if a law had in fact been broken. As you can imagine we get a fair number of domestic dispute calls which turn out to just be someone playing the horse's ass.

Totally.

Eventually, I got involved, when it was finally determined that according to the father he had instructed his ex-wife, the boy's mother, to have their son back in time for an aunt's birthday party which was to take place at two that afternoon. It was her failure to show up that prompted the call in the first place. However, once the father was questioned he confirmed what I already suspected, the agreement stated that visitation ended at six o'clock. Therefore, because there was no clear direction from the State of North Carolina to have that boy back any sooner, I made the decision to hold off issuing a missing child report until after that time, if and when he wasn't brought back.

That sounds reasonable, but doesn't the order allow for extenuating circumstances?

You mean the kind that would require a non-custodial mother to have their son back to his father's in time for an aunt's birthday party? I don't think so. You see that's the problem here, you're only thinking of this from one point of view. What you've heard from Mr. Meade. You're missing a whole other side of the story.

You have an obligation to report a missing child.

And I did, once his disappearance had been validated.

Mr. Meade told me that he had, before speaking to your department, tried calling her and even driven by her place. He grew alarmed when he neither heard from nor saw any sign of them.

That's true. I believe he did exactly that. What's your point?

My point is that the father believed then that his son was in danger of being taken.

Perhaps. We'll never really know will we? The more likely scenario is that Mr. Meade was just out to ring his ex-wife's bell for not following his direction. I think you know that.

It doesn't matter what I know. What matters is how could you have known that then?

I didn't. But policemen, like reporters, I imagine, are often required to follow their hunch.

Your hunch was wrong.

And so it was. Listen, here are the facts. My department, my deputies, did nothing wrong. Hang me if you like for not calling it into the Center for Missing Children right away, but you need to leave them out of it. It was my decision and mine alone.

It just seems like a lot of trouble, for him, calling it in, filing a complaint, driving by her place, all in an effort just to piss off his ex-wife.

There's plenty I know who've done worse.

Barber looked down at his coffee, which he hadn't touched. He poured a couple of spoonfuls of sugar into it and took a drink and then added some more. You mentioned there were two parts to this story, he said.

I did. The other part has nothing to do with this. I don't even know why I should tell it other than for the hope that it might help a young person such as yourself, as it has me throughout my career.

Monroe looked around the diner. He took a drink of coffee and he looked back at the reporter. Some twenty-five years back, he said, you probably weren't even out of diapers then, I'd just started with the department. I was working patrol in the northern part of the county and there was this Lieutenant we had on the force back then, who worked in Detention Services. His name was Bob Winkle, but everybody called him Bullwinkle after that moose from the comics. Anyway, Bob was probably in his late thirties, early forties. Huge fella, arms the size of tree trunks. just the kind of deputy you'd want overseeing prisoners.

Only thing is he wanted to drive patrol, that was his dream of being a deputy. Being out there, helping people, not babysitting locked up criminals. But Bob was fairly new to the department. He'd transferred from somewhere else, I don't remember where, but he was there now and he had to start somewhere and that somewhere was in Detention.

So one day I was out on driving my route, way up near the state line and I spot him in his cruiser weaving all over the road. I didn't know it was him at first, not until I read the car number. I just watched a few minutes from a distance and then thinking I started thinking something was definitely wrong so I pull up behind him and give a little flash of my blue lights, just to let him know I was there. Like I said, he worked in Detention. There was no reason that I could see for him to even be up that way, much less driving like a crazy fool.

Thinking Bob would pull over once he saw my car, I backed off, but he didn't. His driving was very erratic at this point and I remember thinking then that this might be some other kind of trouble, the liquid kind, if you know what I mean. So I radio it in and the dispatcher tells me to pull him over. They said they'd send backup on account of Bob's size. So I did just that. I turned on the lights and the siren and I proceeded to pull old Bullwinkle over. My heart was beating like it'd never had before. Pulling over another officer for DWI. That's not something you do everyday.

Well, it turned out I didn't need to cause Bob must have seen my lights and got distracted and he ran his car off the road and into a ditch. I parked behind him and got out and looked up and down the road, but of course the backup hadn't gotten there yet, so I walk up to Bob's car alone, not sure whether I should be expecting trouble or not. He's sitting there with his head kind of slumped back against the seatback and I call out to him, Are you okay, but he doesn't answer.

About that time, the other car shows up. It's the sergeant on duty. He gets out and walks past me without saying a word and looks in the window at Bob and then flings open the door and hauls him out by the collar. I got the feeling right away these two had had words before. The sergeant, his name was Rhodes, tells me to get the field sobriety kit. I'm just standing there looking at him. Rhodes is trying to get Bob to stand up on his own, but he keeps leaning over. He tells me again and I get the kit and come back and by then Bob has come somewhat to his senses and says he'll not be taking any sobriety test for God or anyone else. He said something about needing to test his sugar, but to me, the way he was slurring his words, it sounded like he was just trying to figure a way out of this mess. I don't know what Rhodes thought, he never said. He asked again and Bullwinkle told him to go to hell and tried to get back to his vehicle, but he slipped in the grass and fell.

Rhodes slapped the handcuffs on him and got him to his feet and ordered me to open the door to his car. I was walking over to check out inside Bob's cruiser for anything that might suggest what was going on, find evidence of his drinking or something, but Rhodes barks at me again and so I did what he asked and opened the door and he shoves Bullwinkle in the backseat. He looks at me and tells me not to say a damn word to nobody about nothing and he leaves. Takes him downtown to a holding cell and they charge him with DWI. Meanwhile, I went back to Bob's car and conducted a search of it and you know what I found?

Nothing, that's what. Not a bottle. Not a can. Not any single thing to suggest he'd been drinking. There wasn't even a whiff of alcohol in that cruiser. What I did find, though, in the glove box was a tiny little black kit. In it was a syringe, a vial of liquid, which I didn't know then but do now know to be insulin, and there was also an electronic metering device and a lancet. I grabbed the bag and headed back into town, thinking I'd struck gold.

You might already know where this is headed, you seem a lot smarter than me, but all I could think of at that time was that he was high on some kind of drugs. You also can probably appreciate how fast word travels in a small town. By the time I get to the jailhouse, Bob has collapsed into unconsciousness and half the town has heard of his arrest. Including his wife, who rushes down to the police station just as the paramedics arrive. She pushes her way through them and injects him in this leg with a shot of something that probably saves his life.

It was hypoglycemia, Barber said.

That's right. Hypoglycemia. A medical condition brought about by his diabetes.

So what happened then?

What could happen? Rhodes got reprimanded. They dropped all of the charges against Bullwinkle of course, promised to forget all about it, let bygones be bygones, that sort of thing. Except for one thing.

He never got to drive patrol.

You got it.

They said his medical condition prevented it.

So Bob tells them what's the point then and quits. I don't know what became his dream then. Not dying, I guess.

Monroe finished and he looked across the table at the reporter. He took a drink of coffee and picked up the bill Marjorie had left and scooted to the edge of the booth

I know you're probably thinking to yourself that's a strange story to tell and I suppose it is. It might only mean something to me, but I told it because I think it's important you should know it's the one thing I think about every single time someone is accused of breaking the law. Rushing to judgement, Mr. Barber, has the potential to do much more harm than good. I hope you'll remember that.

-Anna

The four of them sat gathered around her kitchen table. Alfredo had stopped and bought coffee on his way in from the airport and they listened as Anna told them of her encounter with the lady from the Consulate's Office. As she spoke she kept looking over at where Oliver lay on the floor playing with the extra balloons left over from the papier-mâchè lantern they were making.

But why would your principal request such a thing? asked Giovanni.

I don't know why. He seems upset with how I got the job.

She looked at Alfredo.

We can't help that now, he said.

Could he be working with someone else?

I doubt it, said Alfredo. Not with Evan anyway. If he's found out, he's found out some other way.

Your mother then? said Tore. Perhaps she told him.

She couldn't, said Alfredo. She didn't know. And I spoke to her the day before, she was wary even of him coming around. She would not tell him even if she knew.

You spoke to her? Anna asked.

I have not told you even this, he said. The sheriff of the town in North Carolina, he came to see her. He told her that Evan had hired a private investigator.

He told her that? Why?

I don't know why. Alfredo stood and went to the window. He looked down below on the piazza. But we should consider the probability that whoever is behind this Embassy request is involved also in wanting to steal Oliver back to the US.

Steal him? Anna said.

Alfredo looked at her. That is how it is done.

But what about me?

They will not take you, he said. They come only after Oliver.

How can that happen?

It has happened before.

What can be done to stop it? asked Tore. He was looking at Anna.

There is one thing, answered Alfredo. We must assume they are watching already though.

They looked at him. He looked at Anna.

Go on, she said.

You could do it again, he said.

Disappear?

Yes.

And go where?

Alfredo didn't answer.

Is there no one here who can help, some officials? asked Giovanni.

There is one person, Alfredo said, speaking to Anna. But you will not like who I say.

-Evan Meade

When he landed in Florence it was nine in the morning. Once he went through customs he stopped at a money exchange counter and bought euros and then at the gift shop next door where he found a pocket sized tourist map of the city. Then he made his way outside and waited in line for a cab.

He handed the driver the pink sports bag and a card with the name of the place where he wanted to go scribbled on it in his own handwriting and the driver read it and nodded. With haste he stowed Evan's bag in the trunk and opened the door and Evan sat down. He watched out the window as they went, following along on the map.

People were everywhere, many of them walking briskly, others strolling leisurely in pairs or in threesomes, sometimes enormous groups of them boarding and de-boarding buses, pausing to wipe the sweat from their brows or to look through the lens of their camera at a church or a building or some other tangible proof of their eyewitness to this preserved ancient history, which seemed to him not so much timeless as it was a prisoner to halted progress. He learned to tell quickly the difference between the local Italians and the tourists by their posture and the way they were dressed in shorts and tee-shirts, their heads draped through the straps of every sized camera you could imagine and their bags or haversacks clutched in front of their person to guard against the many warnings from tour operators of the pickpockets and how they walked always looking at this or that or a map, never at what was in front of them, never at where they were headed and he wondered as they came to the one place where he was fairly certain Anna and Oliver had been how in all of this chaos and heat and gloom they, but his son especially, had adapted their lives to this foreign life.

They pulled over to the side of the street and Evan paid the fare and got out. He collected his bag and crossed the street and passed through a small garden to the broad carriage path leading up the hill and then he passed beneath the gate and came to the pool where the statue of Neptune stood. He took from a pocket in his coat the photo of them he'd found at Elena's house and he held it up to compare it to the fountain. Then he slipped it back in his pocket and turned and walked back to the street.

According to the boy on the plane the hotel wasn't far from the northern entrance to the garden, but when he arrived at the front desk to ask for a room they told him none were available. He studied the map before going back outside and hailing another cab.

The University, he told the driver.

Che campus?

I don't know which campus.

C'è Polo delle Scienze Sociali, delle Cascine, Accademia di Belle Arti.

Art, Evan said.

Si, si. Arte.

They drove across the river and made their way to the other side of the city. The driver dropped him off at a hotel across from the entrance to the school and Evan checked into the hotel and took the elevator up to the third floor and once inside his room he laid the bag on the bed and went to the window and opened the drapes and stood looking out on the square below wondering where he should start first.

-Monroe

When he got to the office the next morning it was earlier than usual and Stokes was the only one there. Monroe walked in and set his thermos of coffee down on the desk and turned and asked from the doorway if there'd been any calls?

No sir. None yet. The deputy looked at the radio. I imagine the crime machine will start up soon enough though.

Monroe looked at him a moment and wanted to say something about the youth of today but he just shook his head instead and went back inside his office and sat down. He looked at the phone. What are you waiting on? he mumbled.

What's that, Sheriff? Stokes called from the counter

Nothing.

Monroe reached over and picked up the phone and dialed a number he read off a business card. He waited, then he hung the phone up. Stokes, he called.

There was the squeaking of the chair, boots scrambling across the floor, and then the deputy stood in the doorway. Yessir, Sheriff?

I need to get hold of Agent Bob Forster at the FBI office in Charlotte. See if you can't find me his direct number will you?

Sure thing, Sheriff.

Monroe looked at his watch. He took out his mobile phone and wrote a text to Rebecca. Within seconds his phone vibrated. He read what she wrote back and put it away.

Here's the number, Sheriff. The deputy stepped in and handed him a slip of paper. It was in Jeannie's rolodex.

Nice work. Stokes stood there looking at him. Thank you, Monroe said and the deputy turned and left and Monroe picked up the phone and spent the next few minutes bringing the agent up to date.

This come as a surprise to you? Forster asked.

Nothing surprises me anymore.

I wished you'd have called me sooner. Might have been able to stop him at an airport.

That about sums up the story of my life. Monroe hung up and dialed the number again off the business card.

Global Investigation, a girl's voice answered.

This is Sheriff Monroe Rossi. Can I speak to Carl Demski.

I'm sorry, Sheriff. Mr. Demski's not here.

When will he be?

He's traveling, sir. I'm not sure how long he'll be away.

Would you mind telling me to where?

Sorry, Sheriff. I'm not at liberty to say. If this is an emergency though I can reach him for you. He can call you right back.

I'd like that, please.

Their plans had been for dinner, not lunch, but he asked her if she wouldn't mind changing and she had agreed. So he picked her up at the school in third period and they drove over to what had once been a favorite place of hers to eat with him during the summertime vacation. He parked out front and they got out and walked in and sat down at the counter on a pair of the colored swivel stools. The girl behind the counter came up and they ordered off the same painted menu board that'd been hanging on the wall for the past forty years.

Monroe looked over at Rebecca. He said, Thank you for coming today.

She nodded. It's like playing hooky, but with permission.

How's school.

It's fine.

Volleyball?

I wish it was over.

Not as much fun as you thought it'd be?

No.

You ever think about quitting it?

Why?

I don't know. If you're not happy.

Would you want me to?

It's not my decision.

No, but what would you think about it.

I'd want whatever you want.

She looked at him. You feeling all right? she asked.

He laughed. Why?

I don't know. You just don't sound like yourself. All this talk of quitting and doing whatever it is I want.

Not whatever, he said. I didn't say go do whatever you want. I just asked had you thought about quitting.

Well the answer's no. I haven't.

The girl brought them their waters. She said their hotdogs would be right up and walked away. Monroe took the little bit of paper off the straw and took a sip.

There's no shame in it, if you did, he said.

I never thought there was.

Can I ask you something?

Sure.

You never thought much of me being sheriff, did you.

Is that a question or a comment?

I meant it as a question.

She looked down at her drink. Did I think much of it?

Yeah. I mean it must have been hard on you.

It was. It still is.

You think I should quit?

She looked at him. So that's what this is about. It's not me who's thinking of quitting, it's you.

He shrugged. Maybe.

And so you're asking me? Really?

Yeah. I'm asking you.

She looked away again. I think it's like you said, you gotta do whatever you think it is will make you happy, right?

Monroe looked at her without speaking. He was happy just to be watching her.

She felt his stare. What? she asked.

Nothing, he said.

No, it's something all right.

He looked ahead. You just remind me a lot of your mother.

Because of what I said, about it being hard on me?

He shook his head. No, not because of what you said.

Then what?

Because of who you are.

Rebecca picked up her glass of water and took a drink and she set it back down on the wet ring on the counter.

Don't take that the wrong way because we're divorced. I loved your mother, he said. Part of me still does.

His phone went off and he reached down and silenced it. It was, he later discovered, the private investigator's office calling to confirm his suspicion that Demski had gone to Italy.

Don't you need to get that? Rebecca asked.

He shook his head. It can wait, he said.

The waitress brought them their food.

How's Grandpa? Rebecca asked.

Feeling better. Still doesn't want to be at that place where he's living.

He tried anymore to leave?

Nope. Not that anyone's told me.

You think he will.

Yes, he said. I think he will.

What are you going to do?

I don't know.

They ate. When they were almost done, Rebecca asked: Have you talked with her?

He looked at her. Your mother? Yes, he nodded, we've talked.

About what?

You, he said.

And what else?

Her.

Rebecca smiled. What did you talk about me?

We talked about what a good kid you've been and how you are growing exactly into the person you need to be. We talked about how proud we are of you.

She studied him and then turned away.

I just wanted you to know that, he said. Don't ever think that you've let me down, because you haven't.

She looked at him again and she started to say something but stopped. She lowered her eyes to the table. When she looked up again, there were tears in them. People are talking, she said. They say they saw your car over at that librarian's place.

He watched her, then he looked away. I'm sorry, he said. I should not have let that happen.

What's there to be sorry for, she said. Those people are just saying things to be mean, to pick fun of you.

Probably so.

Well, you know what I told them? I told them to fuck off.

He smiled and looked at her and she put her hand on his arm. He patted her hand. I love you, he said.

I love you, too, Daddy.

They finished eating and afterwards he drove her back to the school. He stopped out front at the steps and put the car in park. Rebecca opened her door to get out, then she turned back around and said, And by the way, it's not been that bad.

What hasn't?

Being a sheriff's daughter. I know you think I think that, but I don't. Sometimes I do, but not really, not often. You know what I mean.

Yes, he answered, I certainly do.

-Anna

She took down the papier-mâchè balloon where it had been hanging overnight taped by the string to the cabinets to dry and she carried it over to the table where Oliver was waiting.

What's next? he asked. He was wearing one of her long sleeve shirts she had given to him for an art smock.

Next we pop the balloon.

Can I do that?

Sure. She handed him the scissors. Just be careful, she said. That's it. Don't cut the tissue paper.

Oliver punctured the balloon and it burst and he jumped and the two of them laughed. She took the scissors and then the project from his hands and she reached through the hole in the bottom and gently pushed the sides of the lantern back out until the balloon released from where it was stuck inside and removed it.

Now, she said, we just need to flatten this out a bit. She pushed it down against the tabletop. There, she said when she was happy. See? Now it stands up on its own.

Do we light it now? Oliver asked.

Not yet, she said. That comes later. Would you like to decorate it?

He nodded and she went and got the box of paint where she'd set it out in the windowsill earlier in the day. She placed it down in front of him.

I can paint it, he said.

Not paint, she replied. Too messy. I thought we'd make handprints.

She doled out some green paint onto a paper plate and helped him roll up his sleeves and then she lowered his hand into the paint.

It's warm, he said smiling.

It's been setting in the window.

She picked up his hand and held him by the wrist and told him to spread his fingers wide. Then she asked him to close his eyes.

Close them why?

Just do.

He did as she asked and she softly touched his hand to the tissue lantern. When she pulled it away there was a little green handprint left behind.

Now open them, she said.

He looked at his handprint and he smiled at her and he smiled at the palm of his hand covered in green. He asked: Can I do it again?

Go wash your hand in the sink first. We'll do a different color.

He went running into the kitchen and came back drying his hand with a hand towel. I want to do blue this time.

After he'd made a couple of more handprints, he looked over at her and asked, Aren't you going to make one too?

This is yours. You can do it.

It's ours, he said. And I want you to.

All right. She pushed up her sleeve.

What color do you want it? he asked.

I don't know. What do you think?

I think yellow.

Why yellow?

I don't know. It makes me think of you. Like the sun.

Okay. She let him take her hand and ease it down into the yellow paint. He pushed down gently on the back of her hand, making sure the paint oozed up into all the creases. Doesn't that feel like the sun? he asked, then he whispered into her ear: Just pretend.

It feels just like it, she said and when he looked up at her she winked.

He lifted her hand and guided it over to just above the tissue lantern. Ready? he asked.

I'm ready, she said.

Close your eyes, he said and she closed them.

She felt his little fingers on her arm and at her wrist and she wished for that instant that time would stop. That they were alone in this world together, and if ever there was a heaven this is what it would feel like. The warmth of the sun at her fingertips and a child's guiding touch.

-La Festa della Rificolona

The two men, one of which was the investigator Carl Demski, were sitting outside at the small corner bakery across the piazza watching the apartment. The other one was wearing a baseball cap and reading a book. He had been there now for a couple of days and because of that knew where in the piazza was the best to sit and not be noticed but still have a good line of sight on the entrance to the building. Sitting on the table before them was an expensive digital camera, two paper cups and an empty bottle of water.

Demski was reading the paper. He had purchased it that morning from the newspaper stand nearby. The Italian vendor, who would step out of his stand every now and then and look their way, had seemed very interested in where he was visiting from. Demski had told him California.

The waiter came up and offered to take their trash and the man in the hat handed it to him. He said something else to the boy and they both looked at Demski, who folded the newspaper and nodded. The boy went away and returned a moment later carrying two coffees to go.

The two men got up and Demski handed the boy some money and slung the camera around his neck and they headed across the piazza and into a clothing store where one of them could always been seen looking out the shop's windowfront.

Evan, too, spent the day out amongst the comings and goings of the city. He had no clear agenda with where he went, only that to find her would require he know where to look. How he had even come to know they were there was because his only other visit to the city was during the last two days of a hurried weeklong vacation, that followed oddly enough his wedding to Angela. She had been obsessed with taking pictures of statues then and looked for clever ways to photograph them. But he, however, then and now, longed for the retreat as soon as he stepped out into those crowded, narrow streets. Florence, he thought, was a dirty backwater town filled with the dusty relics of an age he cared nothing about.

Most of the morning he'd spent squandering in and around the gardens near the Neptune fountain because that was all he had to go by. It was foolish of him to think she'd come back there but you never knew what habits people developed when they were on the run. It had brought him good luck so far. By mid-afternoon however he finally sat down on a park bench near a school determined to think things differently. What would you need? Public transportation. Someplace busy. Near a school. He stared at the empty playground behind the black iron fence. You'd have to work, wouldn't you?

He took a bus back to his hotel in the north part of the city and he stopped at the front desk and asked for a phone book. The boy behind the counter spoke English and he inquired about the city schools.

Which one? There are hundreds, the boy said.

Any where Americans would go?

There is the International School. It is junior through upper grades.

For the younger students too?

Yes, yes. All age of students go there.

How far is it from here?

It is south of the river.

What time do they let out?

Around this time, but schools are closed today.

Why?

For the Festival of the Rificolona.

Evan was quiet a moment. He looked up at the boy. Where might an art teacher go to teach?

Please, Signore, the boy smiled. This is Florence. Art is taught everywhere.

Evan went back outside and stopped. There was a small group of students coming up the sidewalk and he stepped aside to let them pass and behind them came a family of four. A man and woman and two young children. Both were carrying colored paper lanterns at the end of a long stick and singing a song. They passed and he turned and followed.

Anna was standing at the window holding the curtain back and watching the piazza below where Giovanni was closing his shop. When he finished he glanced up in her direction and tipped his hat and walked away.

Can we go yet? Oliver asked.

She let go of the curtain and turned and looked at him. He was holding his Disney backpack by the straps and standing by the door, his paper lantern dragging on the floor. She walked over and took it from him. Do you want it ruined before we ever even have the chance to light it?

Are we going?

Soon, she said and she laid the lantern on the table and walked back to the bedroom and got her jacket and a leather bag of her own with a long strap that she could put her head through and she came back into the main house. She helped Oliver into his and gathered her purse and a paper shopping bag she had filled earlier in the day and then walked over and opened the door to the hall.

Mom, the lantern.

She went back for the lantern and handed it to him and said, Be careful with it, and they stepped into the hall. She closed and locked the door behind her.

Can we take the elevator? Oliver asked.

He pushed the button and watched for the small elevator to come up the shaft and when it stopped he pulled open the iron gate and slid back the door and stepped inside. Anna came in behind him and closed them in and he looked at her and she nodded and he pushed the button.

When they reached the ground floor he opened the door and the gate and rushed for the exit. Wait, she called out and he did. She took his hand and they went out into the piazza and down to the corner and to the bus stop where she purchased two tickets from the orange kiosk.

They waited with a group of other travelers. Tourists and locals alike. A couple with two young children who carried their own macabre lanterns. Oliver looked at the elaborate design and then he looked at his own and he looked up at his mother and smiled. Anna smiled back at him.

The bus came and they boarded at the rear entrance and took the first two seats together and sat looking out the windows until it reached the Bapistry where they got off. They moved out of the way and two men brushed past her, one of them wearing a baseball cap. She watched them until they stepped over the pedestrian chain into the piazza and then she led Oliver by the hand up the cobbled street to where they stopped near one of the entrances to the cathedral.

Behind them on the steps stood a small chorus of children dressed in costume and singing: Ona, Ona, Ona, O che bella Rificolona, La mia l'é coi fiocchi, La tua l'é coi pidocchi!

What are they singing? asked Oliver.

It's a song about the lanterns.

What does it say?

It says mine is tied with bows and yours has lice.

What's lice?

A nasty little bug.

Why are they singing about that?

Because they're poor.

Oliver watched them. Are we poor? he asked.

She looked at him. Do you feel poor?

He shrugged. I don't know. What's does it feel like?

Like you have very little to be happy about.

Oliver thought about it. He picked at some dried glue on the lantern. Did you ever feel that way? he asked.

Not now I don't, she said.

But did you ever?

Once upon a time I did, she said.

When?

Not so long ago.

The crowd started moving and she said to him, Let's go, and they worked their way into the forward progress of a small group of people who were shuffling slowly up the road in the shadow of the great dome. They passed some outside diners and souvenir stands and came past the Museo dell'Opera where in its courtyard Michelangelo had created David and she thought that of all the great many things in this city she would have liked to have shown her son it was that and she thought of the other places where the great artists and craftsmen had labored and toiled over their work and she wondered how after this night she might never again have the chance.

They turned down a narrow side street and merged with the larger crowd being led by a bishop. Oliver saw that other children had their lanterns lit and he asked for her to light his. She said that she would when they came to a good place to stop. His arms were tiring and he was starting to let the lantern dip closer and closer toward the heads of the people walking to the side or in front of them. She kept reaching for him to hold the stick upright.

I can do it, he said.

I know you can. Just hold it up straight.

I know.

A group of boys ran past them and a moment later some child up ahead of them in the crowd squealed and the procession stopped. She pulled Oliver to the side. Here then, she said to him, let me light it.

He lowered the stick and she took the lighter from her coat pocket and reached in through the opening at the bottom and carefully touched the flame to the votive she'd glued to a cardboard platform.

Please be careful with it, she said.

Oliver lifted the stick and she showed him again how to hold it. They joined the crowd in that manner then, repeating the century old steps of the poor country farmers and their families.

Where do we go? he asked.

We just follow everyone else.

Evan had stopped to eat a slice of pizza at a place that had outdoor seating and when he finished the last of his beer he stood and walked out into the street and fell into step with the passers by. It was dark now. In the distance the sound of a large gathering. A jubilant crowd.

On his left passed a group of young rowdy boys darting along the outer edge of the procession and he watched as they stopped and took aim with ornate wooden tubes pressed to their lips and pelted the lanterns with spit wads of paper. One round lantern shaped like the sun with a painted-on face erupted in flames just in front of them and they laughed and whooped and congratulated one another and just as quickly moved on. Others were laughing as well and no one, other than the small female owner of the torched lantern, seemed to mind.

The procession entered the square and Oliver pulled on her arm and pointed to the statue of the equestrian rider, Ferdinand, that stood near the center of the piazza, where a small bonfire had been lit. There were other fires too, at the entrances to the church and the cloister, and she pointed them out to him and said, Let's try that way first.

She rested her hands on his shoulders and guided him to the right. They came to the steps of the old orphanage, which now was the Ospedale, and they made their way up the steps and stopped and stood with a group of others beneath the arched loggia. She looked at her watch.

Mom.

She looked at Oliver. His candle had gone out. She asked him to lower it and he did and she peered in through the slit in the paper and looked at the candle. It's burned down, she said.

I know.

No, it's gone. The wax is melted. There's nothing left.

Oliver frowned. He set the end of the stick on the ground and walked it forward so as to look inside it himself. Did you bring another one? he asked her.

No, she said. I thought that one would last. I'm sorry.

More people were coming up the the steps and she grabbed Oliver by the jacket and gently pulled him further back behind the crowd.

I can't see back here, he said.

She didn't answer, nor did they move. She was studying the wall. Had Tore not told her of it she would not have even noticed the small rota located in the far corner. But it was there. A tiny revolving door. Centuries ago, it had been used to receive children anonymously so parents could come anytime of the day or night and in secret turnover their unwanted children to those behind the orphanage's operation. It was desertion of the quietest and most modest of sorts.

Beyond the arched loggia the crowded square grew suddenly quiet. She stood on her toes and looked above the head of those in front of them and watched as everyone turned to look at a lone figure standing in the center of the square on a small platform raised near the statue of the horse and rider. The bishop was dressed in an olive wool habit and though she tried to hear what he was saying there was no microphone and the distance was too great to make any sense of his words. Moments later everyone's heads bowed.

At that moment, to the right of the bishop a tiny inferno erupted as one of the lanterns suddenly caught fire and there was laughter as the papier-mâché burst into flames.

Anna looked again at the rota and she looked down at Oliver and squeezed his shoulders until he looked up at her. She whispered into his ear. There's something I want to show you, she said.

What?

It's a secret.

He looked at her.

Come on, she said and he let her lead him over to the door where a small sliver of a light shone through a crack. It was almost enough to see inside to the other side.

What is it? he asked.

A tiny door.

Where does it go?

Excuse me.

Anna turned and looked up at the sound of a voice she'd been fearing since she'd driven off with him months ago. An American man stood in front of them. Tall. Thin dark hair. He was one of the two men she had seen getting off the bus.

The American looked down at the boy. You must be Oliver, he said.

Evan was about to step down from the concrete pile when after the excitement with the burnt lantern died down he noticed two men standing in the light beneath the arched loggia. One of them Demski. The other he did not know. When the two men suddenly started to move with a purpose, Evan looked ahead of them and scanned the crowd, searching the faces for whatever it was that had motivated them. But he knew without seeing what it was. He could not see well so he stood higher on the tips of his toes and then stepped up on the rail encircling the statue. He saw them. Anna first, then Oliver. Standing beneath the arched ceiling, moving slowly with their backs against the wall. Oliver was carrying a stick like all the other children, with a paper lantern affixed to one end as his mother was ushering him along.

A carabinieri came over and tapped the metal bar with his baton and Evan looked at him and he made motion for him to get down. Evan did and started his way through the crowd. Maneuvering amongst them. Trying unsuccessfully to keep Anna and the two men in his sights. Giving that up, he aimed himself simply in their general direction, the crowd tightening around him then loosening again as he made for himself a hole.

Anna stood facing the men. She nudged Oliver behind her. What do you want? she asked.

Demski answered. You know why we're here.

He's not yours to take.

We're not here to ask. His voice was kind, almost compassionate. Not at all what she had pictured in her mind.

The one in the ball cap had put some space between he and his partner and she looked at him and told him to stop and he looked at her. She reached behind her and took Oliver's pole from him and she held it up with one hand. She glanced toward the two carabinieri standing not far away at the main entrance to the hospital.

There's no reason to turn this into something ugly, Demski told her.

You're not taking my son.

Anna was standing directly in front of the rota and she felt the door push open against her leg. A hand brushed her pants cuff. She looked at Demski. Then she took a step forward as if to make her way past them and when she did the small door behind her opened fully and she stopped and dropped the stick and swung Oliver around by the straps of his pack and shoved him down toward the door. She saw hands emerge reaching for him. Closing around his arms. Dragging him backwards. He disappeared and the door closed shut behind him. A latch clicked.

Anna stood up and looked at the door. She looked at the two men but all she saw of them was their backs as they were running toward the hospital's main entrance. She turned and checked the door again and was readying herself to leave when something struck her from behind.

The force drove her against the wall and she slammed sidefirst into the plaster stucco. Pain shot down her arm and across her back and shoulders left her gasping for air. She tried to lower herself to the floor but Evan held her pinned to the wall with his knees. His own breathing was heavy and hot where his face was pressed up against her ear. She felt something wet on her cheek and she thought it might be blood. She had yet to even see him, but she knew who it was. She knew.

Where is he? Evan hissed.

She didn't answer.

Where is he?

He pushed off her and with his weight gone she fell to all fours. He stood over her then like some heaving champion. I saw him, he said through clenched teeth. He looked all around them. He was right here.

She tried to get up and he kicked her in the stomach, his foot lifting her off the ground onto her fingertips and the balls of her feet and she groaned and collapsed onto the pavement. She thought she might vomit. He stepped back and she rolled to her side and hugged her stomach. A few seconds passed. When she opened her eyes she could see the soles of his shoes, the pants legs of others, blurry faces in the near distance. Then she felt his hand on her back. He was bent down and crouched beside her. He put his face up close to hers. Where the fuck did you send him?

I'll never tell you, she said.

Evan growled as he started to get up and he reached over and grabbed a handful of her hair. He was just starting to yank her to her feet when the carabinieri's black baton caught him square across the small of his back. He stumbled wincing into the wall.

Anna lay still a few seconds, unsure of what had happened, only that something or someone had caused him to let go of her. When she slowly lifted her chin she turned and looked behind her and saw Evan laying on his side with his back against the wall. The two carabinieri were standing over him. One of them looked at her and came over and took her hand and helped her to feet.

Grazie, she said.

Cosa è succede? he asked.

Niente.

Lei conosce quest'uomo?

She looked in Evan's direction. No, she said.

He told her she was free to go and she thanked him and went about gathering the things she had dropped. Her purse, the paper sack. She looked for but saw no sign of Demski and the other man. When she looked down again at Evan she saw he was looking up at her. She has my son, he said to the one carabinieri standing over him. He pointed. Ask her. She took him.

The officer looked at her. Sono sola, she told them and started to walk away.

Un momento, signora.

She stopped.

One of the carabinieri walked over and he picked up Oliver's backpack and looked at it. He looked at her and then walked over and handed the bag to her. She took it without speaking.

She turned and came down the steps. Faces in the crowd watched her and she walked by. When she turned the corner she passed through a covered walkway to a darkened sidestreet and she made her way quickly down it to a postern in the wrought iron fence and she slipped inside a small wooded courtyard.

She stooped over next to a park bench and reached into the paper bag and took out a wig and a pair of reading glasses and she put them on and tossed the bag aside. She slipped out of the jacket and stuffed it under the bench and straightened the sweater she was wearing underneath it. She gave one final adjustment to the glasses and stepped back out into the street, falling into step behind a small drunken group of university students who were leaving the festival, her son's little backpack swinging by her side.

Evan watched her leave. One of the officers lifted him to his feet and he spoke something to him in Italian and when Evan didn't answer he repeated himself. Non parlo, he replied.

He felt his hands being taken and his arms twisted behind his back and he pulled at them and jerked one free and then the other and he turned his back to the wall and faced the two armed carabinieri. One of them was holding a pair of handcuffs and the other the baton. Wait, Evan said. Then he remembered the word, or a word like it and said, Aspettare. Aspettare.

The officers looked at one another.

I can explain, Evan said.

Behind the carabinieri there lingered a couple and their two young daughters. Each girl was holding a lantern aloft in the air. To the left of them, partially hidden in the crowd, stood one of the boys Evan had spied earlier in the night. The boy lifted the blowgun to his mouth and there was a quick buzz and then a tiny thunk as the spit wad ripped through the tissue paper and struck the candle. In an instant the lantern was engulfed in flames. The girl's sister saw it first and she pointed it out and the older one looked up and saw it and screamed. She swung the lantern in a wobbly arc over her head and then brought it crashing down into her sister's, catching it too ablaze.

The two girls were wailing by now and both of the carabinieri turned to see what the all ruckus was about and when they did Evan turned and ran. He darted down the steps and around the corner and sprinted toward the small gaggle of people stumbling along their way down there.

The group of drunk students turned left toward the University and Anna considered staying amongst them, but that was not part of the plan. The plan called for her to turn right and continue on to their market at Sant' Ambrogio, where was to be reunited with her son and Alfredo, who would take them by car to the coast. Her hip was hurting though where he'd hit her and so she had stopped to rest it and when she did she looked behind her and saw him under the orange glow of a street lamp running toward her.

She stuck with the plan and headed towards the market, passing apartment entrances and garages but nothing that might give her a place to hide. When she came to a narrow side street she stopped and crouched between a row of parked mopeds and peered back down the street but did not see him.

To continue on meant leading him directly to where Oliver was waiting with Alfredo. She would not make it there without him spotting her first. She tested her hip. It hurt but she could go on and she did loping off in the other direction away from the market, away from Oliver and Alfredo, heading south toward the river. Near the corner she ditched the wig and the glasses and stepped out into the middle of the street and she stood watching up the road behind her. It was not long before Evan appeared. She waited and when she was satisfied that he'd seen her she turned down the other street and broke out into a run.

When he saw her she was pretty much standing right out in the open and though a part of him thought that odd he followed after her. She was alone and he wondered still where was his son but what was more important to him at that very moment was how with every step he was gaining ground on her, taking back what had been taken from him, reclaiming what was his. They came to the road that went along the river and Anna slowed. He slowed too and she kept looking back for him and he was always there and it felt good to him for her to know that.

At the arched passageway to the Ponte Vecchio she stopped and turned and looked at him and she looked at the hordes of bystanders, the tourists and jewelry hawkers and souvenir-sellers and they were all there for her as she walked beneath the arches and through the entrance. She went past the vendor stands and out onto the middle of the bridge and she stopped near a bust of some royal member from Florence's past. She leaned with Oliver's backpack still in her hand against the low wall with the river passing below and she waited for him

Evan walked up and stood facing her. Where is he? he asked.

I don't have him.

I can see that. Where is he?

She was surprised by the civility in his voice, as if he were merely a stranger asking directions. He was that way because he thought he had won. She had heard that tone in him before.

You are wasting your time, she told him.

He smiled. Is that so? I found you, didn't I? You didn't think I would, but I did. That doesn't sound like the outcome of someone who's wasting their time.

All you're doing is hurting people.

It's nothing they haven't asked for.

Including my mother?

He looked at her. He didn't answer.

He belongs with me, Evan. You know that. I'm his mother.

You're nothing. You've always been nothing, from the moment you were born.

That's not true, she said softly.

See. Even you have your doubts.

Why did you come here?

You know why I came.

I want to hear you say it.

I came for him.

That's not why.

How do you know?

Because of those two men, the two at the square. You hired them to find Oliver.

Your point?

But still you came. Why?

He looked away. He didn't answer.

It was for me, wasn't it? Look at me.

He did.

They were only ever going to take him back, not me, weren't they? But that wasn't enough for you. You wanted more. You've always wanted something more.

All I ever wanted, he said and then stopped. You ruined it all.

No, Evan. You ruined it yourself. You have only yourself to blame.

She watched him and saw the lines of worry deepen along his forehead and she watched his eyes searching for something he could not see, not ever, and she knew then what he was thinking and just as she started to cry for help Evan lunged and grabbed her about the chest and carried them both over the wall.

Book V

-Oliver

Class ended and the boy stood up out of his seat and slipped one arm through the strap of his Disney backpack. He joined the other students pushing and shoving next to the wall where their coats hung on fat wooden pegs and he found his own and took it down. He followed his classmates out into the long hall. There the afternoon light spilled in through the doors at the opposite end of the corridor and reflected white-gold off the polished floor and the children's gleaming faces.

The children scrambled for the exit, their voices boisterous, riotous almost, and for a moment the boy was nearly lost in that chaotic escape. The doors flew open then and more light poured in and he found his place amongst them and he came through the doors and onto the steps and shielding his eyes from the bright sunlight he made his way down the steps.

A couple of his friends squatted in the dirt nearby to study something they'd found and they saw him and waved. They called him over. The boy raised his hand in return but did not go to them. He adhered strictly to the sidewalk and when he came to the street and the crossing guard he waited until given the signal and then crossed to the narrow stone steps on the other side.

The school sat on a tall pinewood hill high above a rocky shoreline and though he wasn't supposed to run he did. He was careful though to watch his footing on the steep decline, but not so concerned that anyone watching would be alarmed. At the foot of the hill the land leveled out and sloped steadily toward a great cliff overlooking the sea and a tiny secluded harbor.

At the edge of the cliff surrounded by edge ferns and yellow-flowered wood sanicles sat what looked like an old world guard tower. Graying and weathered, but solidly built from stone dredged up by the sea. The restaurant had been remodeled on the inside and according to the man greeting the American couple at the door much was nicer than outside. But they had insisted on a patio table overlooking the tiny harbor. They sat near the railing, sipping espressos from small porcelain cups. On the table were a pair of binoculars and two short glasses of grappa. Their waitress had suggested the liquor when told that their visit was for a celebration.

Strands of the woman's hair rusty red hair stirred in the cool breeze. She brushed it out of her face and looked out over the water. Don't you just love that smell? I feel I could sit here forever.

It grows on you, he said.

You could now, you know?

He looked at her. Could what?

Just sit here, or anywhere else, for that matter.

He thought about that. Well, not quite, but almost. There is this tiny construction project I've got going on out on a certain piece of farm property.

Sure you do. Every sailer has to have a home port to come home to. She nudged him with her elbow and he smiled at her.

Their waitress came up and asked if they liked the grappa.

Monroe looked up at her. She appeared only slightly different than in any of the pictures he had seen of her. Her hair was shorter, and lighter. But the fall from the bridge in Florence had left her apparently with no visible injuries. Only a slight limp when she walked. He looked at his full shot glass. I guess you could say we're waiting for the right moment, he said.

There is no time like the present, she replied.

That's excellent advice, he said and he picked up his glass and he waited for Grace to do the same and he held it aloft and then toasted. To the present.

To the present, Grace said.

They looked at the girl. They waited.

To the present, she replied. And they drank.

Afterwards the girl left and they were both sitting quietly when Grace reached over and caressed his arm. Is that what you imagined it would be?

I don't know what I imagined.

You did good though.

He nodded. He looked at his watch.

Is it time? she asked.

Almost.

She turned and looked around. They were the only ones seated outside. Inside there were just a few others. Two young couples traveling together. She saw the girl standing at a window looking out over the harbor, her arms crossed. She looked at Monroe. How did you ever find this obscure place? she asked.

The old-fashioned way. I asked questions.

Those questions led you here?

They led me to him, he replied and they both looked out over the railing down at the harbor below where figures moved amongst the boats that were tethered to lines or dry docked on the gravel pad and where fishermen stood worrying over poles and equipment and the early season swimmers and sunbathers lay sunning themselves on the harbor seawall.

Your father would love this place.

He never was much for travel. He always thought he had too much to do or it was about the money or him not wanting to leave my mother, even after she died.

It was kind of Carolyn to let him stay with her, and Rebecca, I hadn't even thought of her, she'd love it here too.

Maybe next time, he said.

Yes, next time.

Monroe pointed. Look, here he comes, he said.

She looked at where a young boy had appeared near the boathouse. He was carrying his backpack slung over both shoulders and he walked briskly along the pathway, his eyes searching the men in their boats. He came to the steps leading down to the water and stood there looking out. Suddenly he waved both hands over his head at one of the boats. The boat's lone sailor had already spotted him and had put down the lines and his tackle and taken both oars in his hands. The hatless and bespeckled old man steered the wooden raft over. When he pulled up alongside the steps he stood slowly up from the bench and walked to the front of the boat and he spoke something to the boy. The boy nodded. He took off his backpack and tossed it to him and the old man stowed it beneath the bow. Then he turned back and stood with his feet wide apart to steady himself against the tide's current and he reached his arms out for the boy.

15034395R00150